I0841078

HEART LIKE MINE

Book two of the Heart Series

ALI MARIE

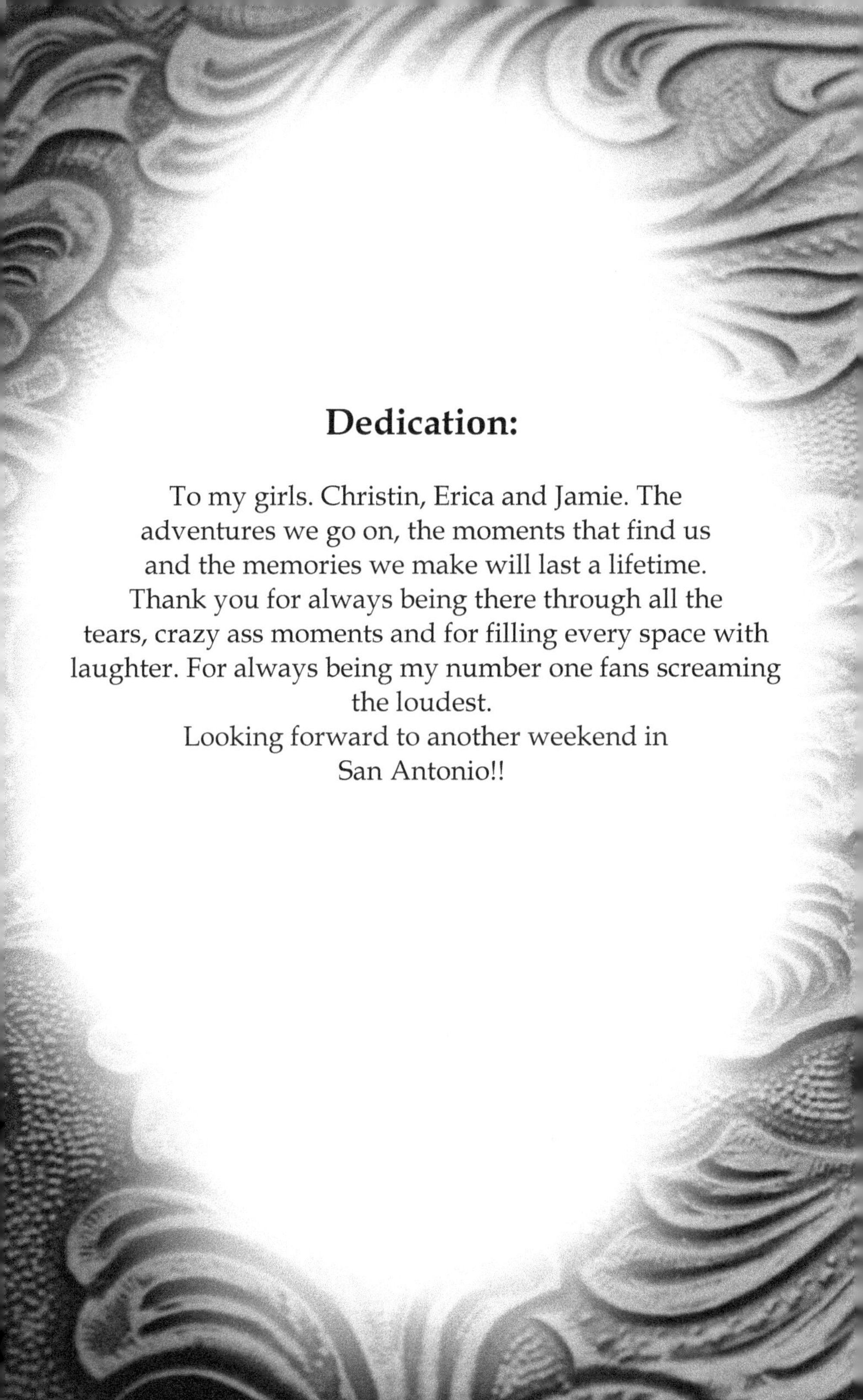

Dedication:

To my girls. Christin, Erica and Jamie. The
adventures we go on, the moments that find us
and the memories we make will last a lifetime.
Thank you for always being there through all the
tears, crazy ass moments and for filling every space with
laughter. For always being my number one fans screaming
the loudest.
Looking forward to another weekend in
San Antonio!!

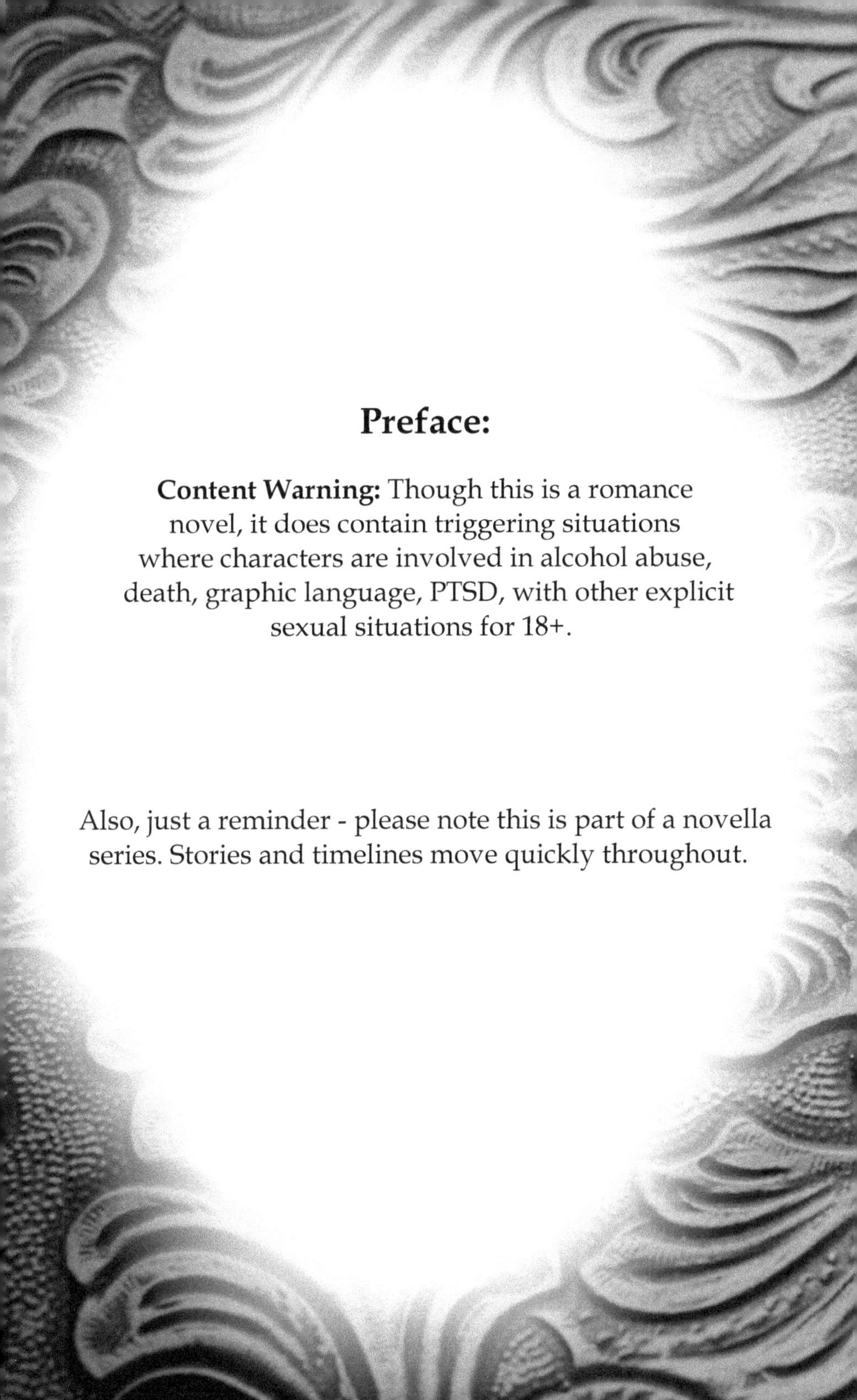

Preface:

Content Warning: Though this is a romance novel, it does contain triggering situations where characters are involved in alcohol abuse, death, graphic language, PTSD, with other explicit sexual situations for 18+.

Also, just a reminder - please note this is part of a novella series. Stories and timelines move quickly throughout.

Playlist:

Pretty Piece of Flesh - Nine inch Nails
Pain - Three Day Grace
River- Bishop Briggs
Middle Finger - Lainey Wilson
Cowgirls - Morgan Wallen/Ernest
Weak-End - Lainey Wilson
Last Night- Morgan Wallen
Bandaid on a Bullet Hole - Morgan Wallen
Crazy - Patsy Cline
Never Say Never - Carly Pearce/Cole Swindell
If I Was a Cowboy - Miranda Lambert
Hate My Heart- Carrie Underwood
Deep End - Priscilla Block
Never Leave - Bailey Zimmerman
Hell & Back - Maren Morris
Can't Help Falling In Love - Kacey Musgraves
Heart Like Mine - Parker Mccollum

PROLOGUE:

Seven Years ago....

I wake in the middle of the bed surrounded by bodies. My head spins with a sharp ache of too much alcohol along with my body aching from too much sex. I laugh to myself, another night in search of pleasure. To feel more than a rotting corpse in my own skin. I shift to move when someone's hand latches onto my calf. "Don't leave yet," she whispers. Another arm of a man pulls me close to his body to cuddle. I think back on a memory seared in my brain. One of many that led me down this path.

I awake with a gnawing pain in my stomach and between my thighs. "What the hell," I moan, finding my hands tied above my head to the bedpost. My eyes fully open to gander over my naked and bruised body. Dry blood cascades down my left breast onto my side then bed sheets. Looking around, I find comfort that I'm in my own room, but then my breath hitches in realization I'm back home, and he is somewhere nearby. That something snapped in him again last night to place me in this position. My mind floods with visions from last night.

"My little whore needs to behave like a dutiful wife. Who are you to tell me what I can and can't do? You came from nothing and now can have the world if you would just. Keep. Your. Fucking. Mouth. SHUT," he spits out in my face. I squirm underneath his body knowing there is nowhere I can go. I'm trapped.

"I didn't mean to tell you what to do. I love you. I just want you safe," pleading.

"You love me, Amity? Huh, I think maybe you once did." He almost looks sorrowful, but then his eyes glass over with intensity. "Let me show you how much I love you." He quickly shreds my clothes off my body, tossing me back on the bed hard enough the breath is knocked out of my lungs when I bounce off the mattress. Then he has my wrists pinned above my head, binding them by rope to the bed. "No escaping me now, my little wildflower." I watch as he strips down, and I notice a few more tattoos since we had last been together, which honestly was only two weeks ago. His body is of a God, face of an angel, but I am believing he may be a spawn of the devil himself. He looks to be carved from stone and then daintily painted on where his tattoos glisten over his skin. I'm a complete fool to constantly be finding myself here with this madman. My skin tingles with the knowledge of this time is different. He is after more than claiming me or punishing me.

The light reflecting off the tip of his knife quickly pulls my attention to focus solely on him. "What are you going to do?"

"I want to watch my wildflower wither underneath me. Let's start keeping a tally of everytime I punish you. When we get to fifteen, I'll up the punishment." His eyes haunted and high as a bear on coke. Far past being in a stable mindset. With those last words, he punctures my skin with the tip of the knife. Dragging it deep and through. All I can do is scream through the twisting pain. "That's right. Scream for me, bleed for me, Amity." When I think he is done cutting me, he pushes his cock into my heat hard and fast. Pounding into my stiff body. I wrath in pain and I hate how my inner core caves to him every damn time, but it's all she has ever known. Even when he knicks my breasts and arms in the process of telling me he loves me, he owns me. At some point, I black out from exhaustion of hours of being fucked, licked, cut, and the pain.

He waltzes in with a tray of orange juice and my favorite breakfast of belgian waffles covered in powdered sugar and blueberries. Placing the tray on the bed, he says, "Here, let me help you. Sorry, I should have untied those before I left to make *breakfast, but you looked so perfect and blissful." I do my best to hide my face of shock. Shock of, who the fuck are you right now?*

"Here let me carry you to the bathroom." I can't even protest before he picks me up, carries me, sitting me down gently on the toilet. In the midst of me peeing, I watch him pull out the saline solution and Neosporin. Once I flush, he picks me back up, sitting me on the cold marble countertop. I watch quietly in horror as he tends to clean every mark he made last night with the solution then applying the Neosporin so it won't scar. "My beautiful wildflower, I made such a mess of you last night. My apologies if I hurt you. But I won't apologize for needing to be embedded in you in every way." He kisses me up my arm, then nuzzles my neck. In this moment, I come to full tuition that I married a fucking sociopath with no escape.

Back to my present life, maybe I should have followed up with a therapist like everyone suggested. Though I think I am doing just fine now. I know how to beat a man's ass if his touch is unwanted, my sweet gullible self no longer exists, and my heart is stone-cold sober. Finding the pain with pleasure was difficult until I found the right people. Now, I indulge in what I want, when I want, as long as it leaves a mark when I'm through.

BLAKE'S PROLOGUE:

We are on the plane for a summer adventure we planned together as friends with benefits only. I can't help but think back to where each of us were a year ago. I find myself chuckling under my breath at how one time, I despised her. Now, here we are. At this moment, she sleeps in a curled-up ball, with her head in my lap. The first time I caught a glimpse of Amity was when she took the stage at one of Paramour's fundraising events. All of who's who in San Antonio was slated to be in attendance. Not really being my brother's kind of scene, I of course represented the Holdings' name with no hesitation. This club showcases luxury and an enthralling sex vibe for all alluring and captivating people in this city. I don't remember the fundraiser cause at all, but her body and voice was embedded into my brain. The local band had been playing a good mix of dance, rock, and country. Then the lead singer invited her on stage, stating he loved her on stage with him as much as he loved to roll in the sheets with her. I'll be honest, he did not strike me as the straightest man in the club, but people surprise me *all the time*.

Before I knew it, some enticing chick strutted up on stage in tight, skimpy red shorts, a black laced corsette that illuminated all her curves, busting breasts, topped off with *fuck me right now* knee-high heel boots laced to the top. I was transfixed on her, even though she was not my typical platinum blonde big boobed bracket. Once the music started, she tossed her long black hair around then started to rock her hips in sync to the beat. Once her mouth opened, everyone in the club screamed for her. Realizing I heard the song, *River* a few times on the radio, her voice owned the song like it was only hers.

Drawing me in, I pulled a few buddies with me as we made our way closer to the stage. I soon had the best view in the house of her sliding on her knees, her hand tantalizing, slowly easing down her body in front me as she sang with fervor. Her voice, raspy and sultry, caused goosebumps to rise over my whole body. I was bound and determined to meet this girl. But once she jumped off stage, she was lost to the crowd. When I found her later in the night, she was sandwiched between some gorgeous blonde and not a bad looking guy making out on their way out of the club. My friend Josh had made some rounds to find out more with not much luck, other than her name was Amity, she frequents the club often, and likes to *play*. In Josh's and my terms, that's code for getting around. I found myself intrigued enough to make the decision to approach her next time I saw her.

The next time was a couple weeks later when she waltzed into Paramour on a Friday night as if she had just come from the rodeo. Hell, maybe she did since she was in tight jeans, a plaid button-up shirt, adorned with a huge-ass sparkling rodeo belt buckle. Not soon after that, she was on stage with the local band of that night, saluting her middle finger. Taking in her more natural vibe, I noticed her face was of a darkened angel with ice for eyes, body petite with her cow-boots, maybe getting her to five-foot-five. Her voice, still raspy and breathless, but haunting and divine. She held the crowd in the palm of her hand, all saluting her with their middle finger. When the song ended, she threw back a shot of whiskey, and I immediately wrote her off as classless. *Nope, that is crazy, waiting to happen.*

Soon, I noticed we were frequenting the same Thursday and Saturday nights. Thursday nights I typically entertain my more eccentric clients who like to indulge in Drag shows, drinks named after sexual acts, and change it up a bit with the spouse. Saturday nights were my night to let loose and find the next new fine piece of ass I could take to my bed. Sometimes multiple. Though I had deemed Amity beneath me, she always drew my attention no matter where she was in the club. It was like I had radar just for her, that would go off when she was near. Over time, she became a nuisance. One night she would roll up in there as if she came from the barn, the next she would ooze sex. Either way, she walked around the club like she owned the place, then I found out she was tight with the owners. But was that inexcusable for the behavior of making out with men and women left and right. Kneeing men in the balls if they touched her, or slap a woman because she was in her space? Now, I don't know the back stories, nor did I care enough back then to figure them out. She annoyed me with her crass mouth that I could sometimes hear over the pumping music. To top all the other bullshit off, this woman would never look my way, regardless of if I was the most handsome and richest man in the room.

The night Nash and Willa found each other, I had taken a glance at the girls with her. They were all beautiful in their own distinct way as they were a palate of hair colors, features, and personalities. Though at a glance, Amity looked familiar that night, but I had other things on my mind and was stoked for Nash, who seemed genuinely interested in someone. Now, the night we all randomly ended up at Paramour together and Willa introduced all of us, I was taken back being that close to Amity. The tension was already building up. Electricity crackled through the air. When we shook hands, the feeling of fire spread through my body so quickly I yanked my hand out of hers. The questionable look on her face told me she had felt something similar. It was at that moment my heart started to beat to hers, and I stayed glued to her side the rest of the night.

The days following that night, Nash gave me the 4-1-1 on Amity along with warnings. She was **OFF** limits. The last thing she needed was a playboy in her life unless I was invited. Per Willa, she was unobtainable unless I just wanted a one-night stand. *Well, I had already gotten her for a few other nights and mornings at that point, so not completely impassable.* Told me Amity likes to dabble in sexual quests, which Nash found amusing because then he thought maybe we would be perfect for each other. Then he remembered I didn't do relationships either. I laughed when he told me most see Amity as a bitch, but that she really is a sweetheart with rough edges. Honestly, I had thought the same thing for months leading up till then. The girl I had been getting to know was adventurous, attentive, took what she wanted, unapologetic, and I found I was the most satisfied when I could make her laugh. Amity has the best heartfelt, charming laugh I have ever heard. Making her laugh has become one of my daily goals along with multiple orgasms. I had soon found myself only wanting to be with her, regardless of the women who tried to lay in my bed. I had an obscene need for her salacious-ness and was becoming more enamored with her each day.

Now I am madly in love with this woman who has undone all sense in my world. Nothing but her makes sense now, and I need to convince her to be mine on this trip. I'm all for rolling in the sheets with others as long as her final ounce of pleasure comes from me solely. But even the sharing is starting to wear on me. I find myself plotting a guy's death when he sinks his dick into her or how can I strangle the blonde when she laps my girl up in ecstasy. I will say though, she only allows me to bring her pain now. Whether that is biting, pressure from my hands, whipping, or whatever she fathoms, she only trusts me. Amity has been a tough cookie to bite into, especially when she wants pain with her pleasure. Over the months, I have slowly been able to dive a little deeper in that head of hers, but not enough to understand where her thought process stems from. I only hope once this trip is over, we find ourselves on an even playing field. I am Blake *Fucking* Holdings, who always takes what I want, receives what I need, and Amity Mercer will be mine.

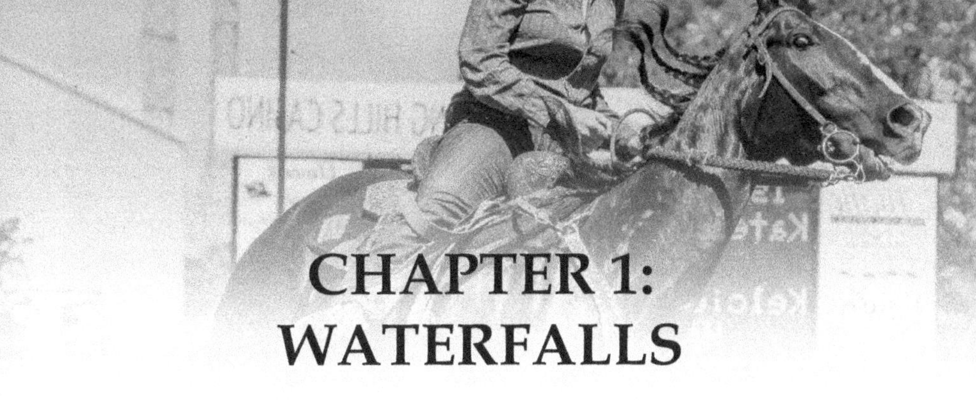

CHAPTER 1:
WATERFALLS

Four months prior…..

"Don't you dunk me, man. I would prefer not dirtying up the last pair of somewhat clean jeans I have with me." All while making sure our horses are tied up but with freedom to graze.

Laughing, Blake stalks toward me with a smirk, telling me I better run and hide or I'm done for. I take off running up the boulders near the waterfall realizing my sense of direction is out to bite me in the ass. Up here, I am going to be trapped. The only way down is past Blake or down the waterfall. *Shit!* "Don't come any closer, Blake. I will not blow you the rest of the time we are here. I swear to it!"

"Amity, come on. You know you can't say no to my pied piper."

"Quit calling it that. We did not agree to that name," I admonish, stumbling backwards up the rocks to keep my eye on him. He lets out a dark, indelicate laugh, inching closer and closer to me.

"Just give in and come here, lemon drop." I roll my eyes at that name. "I'll even carry you down then throw you in. Instead, if you keep moving up these rocks here, we will be jumping off the top." Shaking my head vigorously, my head swirls with ideas to kill him in his sleep. "You better quit thinking of ways to hurt me. Or I'll be tying you up tonight."

"Stop trying to sweet talk me and head back down. You know I'm not a fan of heights anyhow." I've reached the top with nowhere to go but down. Standing close to the edge of the waterfall, my heart is racing as fast as my horse, Nevada, gallops. I feel a tight tug on my ponytail that's hard enough to spin me around, sending me falling into Blake's arms in fear I was about to slip off the edge.

"I got you, bae," he murmurs, running his manicured palms up my arms, then neck until he reaches my face.

"I'm not a fan of that nickname either."
"How about you quit turning down my pet names for you and kiss me?" Before I can deny him, his mouth is on mine. On instinct my arms wrap around his neck, pulling him closer to me. Our tongues dance together while our bodies grind against each other. Lifting me up by my ass cheeks, my legs wrap around his waist. He has my full attention with lust and need for him. My fingers are running through his hair, pulling tightly. Half for passion and half to make him feel pain for tormenting me today. His mouth moves from mine down to and across my cheek bone and neck, and I can feel him harden for me under his jeans.

"Take me now," I whisper.

"Gosh, I wish I could, Tinkerbell, but we have somewhere to be. Get your wings out."
"Aaaaggggghhhhhhhh." *SPLASH!* I swim frantically to the surface, with thoughts of me drowning him dancing through my head. But I don't see Blake when I resurface. "Blake! Blake, where are you?" Panic sets in. That was not that high of a jump, but we did hit the water hard. Dunking my head back in the water, I try to catch a view of him, but it's all churned up from us jumping in. I swim to the closest rock, pulling myself up to look out better. "Blake!" I shout again, frantically looking around.

"Damn, woman, I'm right here." Blake comes swimming up next to me, so I kick my feet to splash water in his face.

"Do not ever do that to me again. I do not want to leave Costa Rica alone and have to explain to everyone you died. They won't believe me that I didn't do it." Chuckling at me, he thinks I'm exaggerating, but he also knows there is truth behind my words. He swims in between my legs to pull my bottom half closer to him as I perch on the rock.

"I'm sorry I worried you. I'll behave for at least the rest of today."

"O peachy keen. You can be such a kid."

"I think someone has her panties in a twist."

"Yah think? They are riding up my ass crack in my jeans."

"Such a Princess." I see a gleam in his eyes as he says the word.

"Don't."

"Don't do what, Princess?"

"Don't call me Princess."

"Oh, by all means, my princess. I'm here to serve." I roll my eyes, knowing there is no changing his mind. He stretches up, kissing my cheek in victory. "Here, slip out of your pants and I will go lay them over there on the rocks to sun dry."

"Fine," I say in a huff. I manage to squirm out of soaking wet Wranglers and pass them off. I look for a smooth section of the long boulder to sit my ass cheeks on, as I adjust my bikini bottoms. Blake swims back over and finds that he can stand up in the water now where I moved to, putting his head up to my chest. He is a tall one for sure, at least six-five. Alluring and sensuous like an Adonis, as my eyes roam over his bare chest and down his rippled abs.

"You checking me out, babe?"

"Hmmmm, maybe. I prefer you with your mouth closed though."

"Oh, do you now? Even when my mouth is doing this?" He sends shivers up my spine placing kisses up the insides of my thighs. Licking my skin in between until he reaches my center. "These need to go." I go to sit up to remove them, but in one swoop, he has the strings on the sides torn apart and tossing them to the shoreline. "Much better, slide down to the edge for me. I'm going to remind you how incredible my mouth is."

His tongue lighty licks up my folds, and already I am on the cusp of losing my mind. Out in the middle of nowhere by a gorgeous waterfall, and any hiker could stop by to see this scene. It just makes this even more intense and exciting. To be caught. To be part of a show for others. I strip my wet top off, letting my breasts free because I know he loves to grab on to them when he is downtown. He instinctively reaches for them with his left hand, sending a moan into my core that vibrates through my whole body. His tongue goes deep with lethal moves as his fingers circle my clit.

My back arches. "Blake, o... O... don't stop." Grabbing a fist full of his hair, pushing him into me. He bends my knees up on the boulder, spreading my knees apart for more access. "Fuck me...sweet love of pineapples."

"Come for me, Amity. Give me what I crave most." He dives back in, lashing his tongue, biting, sucking, then dipping two fingers in me. My core clenches around his fingers as I holler my sweet release, why he kisses and licks me up dry. "I swear Amity, I will never get enough of your sweet pussy. It's my favorite candy in the world." Still catching my breath, he murmurs, "Now I am going to fuck you from behind, so slide your ass down here." He carefully lifts me up toward him then back in the water. The cool fresh water hits my naked body like ice. Feverishly kissing, tasting my candy sweetness on his tongue. His roaming of my breasts, all making me wet again. Soaked again for him. Slowly turning me around, he puts his arm across my waist to hold me up over the rock. With his other hand, he guides himself into my core.

"Blake," I gasp out. He groans by my ear, letting me know I make him come undone. *Literally.* No matter how many times I am treated with his cock, it's a damn Christmas morning surprise every. Damn. Time. Blake bites my earlobe between his teeth before sucking on it. Pulling back just enough to spank my ass, then comes back to drill me harder. Pain and pleasure. Just the way I love sex. The sounds of moans and our bodies slapping together fill the peaceful, serene air.

Close to hitting my precipice, we both hear a gasp. Turning my head to the right, I spot a younger couple who must be out for a nice hike in the rainforest to look at all the waterfalls. They are both frozen in shock as they watch Blake fuck me from behind, relentlessly. I lock eyes with the guy. His eyes never blink or waver from mine. Blake slams my body down on the boulder, taking the arm that was holding me up, to now wrapping my ponytail around his fist.

"Mine," he growls out. "You are mine, Amity." Thrusting harder into me, he yanks my head back with my hair, causing me to arch my back to relieve some of the pain. "They can look, but not touch. No more of anyone touching you." My brain is firing all sorts of alerts as my heart loosens the knots around it. "Tell me you're mine, Amity. Only mine." Grunting at me as I can tell he is close. "Tell me now!"

I shout, "Yes, I'm yours," at the height of my orgasm, milking him for every drop while we both grasp for air for several minutes.

"Fuck. Fuck, are you okay?" Blake asks, panting in my ear. I blink to release the man from my sights, watching the girl drag him off. All I can hope is we gave them some insight, because he looked to be a vanilla tight wad in his yellow crocks and plaid swim shorts.

Turning my attention back to Blake, I murmur, "I'm blissed out. That was, um, that was intense. Where did that come from?"

"I don't know. My instincts are changing. Instead of just pleasing you with every desire, I now want to protect you and be the only one giving you pleasure. I know that sounds crazy and not what we agreed to, but hell." He runs his fingers through his dark blonde hair with natural highlights from the sun.

I blink wide-eyed at him. Should I tell him when that chick was sucking him off last week, it hit a nerve? We have been "seeing each other" for eight months now. Sometimes it has just been us in bed, others we had company. *I'm Amity.* I do not get attached to people unless you are like my best friend ever, and I have three of those already. *Damn, is he one now?* I think back to all the times we just hung out at each other's apartments on the weekend, cooking, watching trashy television, him helping me with grading papers when I got behind, because he is literally in me ALL the time. "I think you are one of my best friends." I blurt out.

He picks me up and twirls me around to hide his disappointment, then carries me over to the shore so we can get dressed. I feel so awkward right now. "Please say something. I didn't mean for that slip. I blame all the sun we've had."

He chuckles softly, almost still unsure what to say. "Give me a minute." Taking my hair down to fix it, I watch him go to his bag and grab a small box.

"Here, this is for you." I stare at him goggle-eyed, looking at him like he grew three heads in the last five seconds. Opening the box, I am blessed with the site of the emerald leather bracelet I had fallen in love with several days ago back into town. When we went back yesterday, it was gone.

"O my Jesus, Blake, you're the one that bought it." I jump into his arms, kissing his face all over. He pushes me back a little bit, holding me steady with his hands wrapped on my upper arms.

"I think I am falling for you, Amity." I gasp. "You don't have to say anything, besides, you already told me I'm your best friend, which I'm still not sure how I feel about."

"Blake, I promise what I said is not a horrible thing. But that I meant; you are one of my favorite people. That I'm somehow attached to you and that I may be falling for you too." His baby blues glimmer, bending down to kiss me with his soft luscious lips.

"You're my favorite person too, peanut."

"Still not feeling the peanut name."

"Why not? You're salty like one, but oh so tasty. Also, I just want a pocket full of you to snack on."

"You're crazy," I say, laughing.

Blake replies, "Apparently crazy about you," taking my face in his palm to pet. Gah, I don't even know what to do with these precarious emotions.

"Let's head back to town so we can wash up and head to dinner. Last night in this town. Next stop Jaco."

"Can't wait, let's go."

One week later…..

"I can't believe we are headed home after a month of traveling through Costa Rica. Let alone on horseback most of the time. It was surreal. Thank you, Blake."

"Anything for my girl." He grabs my luggage from the taxi, and we roll into the San Jose Airport.

"That name I approve of." He flashes me his best smile, causing my heart to skip a beat, and I smile back.

On the flight, I reflect over the last several months with Blake. Though our relationship started out on the unconventional side of things, with two other people in the bed, we had an instant connection. Sure, I had seen him around Paramour before, but never thought he was my type. He always showed up in fancy suits, expensive shoes, and watches. Has a confidence about him that compared to a King of a sovereign country. He exudes wealth and sex. Rumor was he slept with only models, but never the same one twice unless it was an orgy. Deemed the Cassonova of the Holdings brothers. Legit the complete opposite of Nash.

Then when Willa and Nash introduced us, sparks splashed across the sky. That first night we shared ourselves with each and others. There was a possessiveness we encountered though. Not wanting the other to enjoy themselves with another too much. It was without words, but of locking eyes when the other was receiving pleasure. Stepping in at the perfect time to be the cause of heightened ecstasy at the finish line. Even that night, we left my friend's place and went back to Blake's. From there, we built a friendship with incredible orgasms as a bonus. He slowly earned his way into my life. Earned my trust and now my heart. Not by fancy dinners or extravagant gifts, but by just being there. Showing up unprompted. Making me laugh constantly and letting me know the true Blake under all the layers.

Not going to lie, this man can be hot tempered but a gentle giant. I have a theory that Clint received majority of the calmness, and all the *relax the fuck out* genes. Left a little for Nash and not an ounce for Blake. I have found he is spectacular at his job, closing deals, because he is ruthless. Lays all cards out of the table, except the one he keeps up his sleeve. Is cunning and a suave smooth talker. All up until something does not go his way. We've had our arguments of what a prick he can be, with the occasional throwing of objects. Only to relent to hot, angry makeup sex afterwards. I've heard him threaten people on the phone over business deals. Have words with the staff when his expectations haven't been met instead of going with the flow. On the other hand, he has this gentle side that seems to be saved just for me. The soft touch to my arm or lower back. A kiss to the head or shoulder in the middle of a crowd. He always finds a way for us to be touching, regardless of the scene. Speaks poetry to me and sheaths me with compliments. Many occasions I have called him a mutant, which is the extreme alternative to the *Diva Bitch* name he gets daily.

This past week, he told me I grounded him. Checked him on his bullshit without fear of repercussions. Blake has had to learn; I am not a woman that rolls over to spread my legs for a good time. That my backbone is stronger than his, and I have no problem handling my shit. Which, he has had to teach me to soften a little and allow him to do things for me and pay for things. Like this trip. When I agreed to go, I stated I would buy my own ticket. He countered that his company has a private jet. I refused to stay at high-end resorts, so we compromised on two to three nights a week. We would indulge the resort life so he could be pampered. The rest of the time we would backpack to hostels or camp outside. Then we would trade off buying food and drinks. One, we weren't a couple, and we do the same thing at home. Two, I didn't want to feel like I owed him anything. At the time or later down the road for whatever our relationship was, and it didn't last. Not a week into our trip, he managed four resort days, and somehow, we left every meal without me paying. I've come to learn, Blake Holdings always gets his way.

Finally landing back home in San Antonio, I say, "Home sweet home."

"Back to reality, Nash sent me a text. I need to be in his office by nine Monday morning."

"Ouch! That sounds rough. I'm sure all's fine, though. My summer school class does not start till Tuesday, so I will be thinking of you cozying in bed with Hamlet."

"You know he is my dog, right?"

"Is he though?" Giving him a wink, I start laughing. He titters, knowing damn well the black oversized rescued newfie named Hamlet now prefers me over him these days.

"At least we have the weekend to recover. Your place or mine?" he asks.

"I probably need to check my mail. Want to hang at mine tonight so I can start laundry then switch to yours tomorrow?"

"Sounds like a plan if that is what will make my girl happy."

"So happy," I whisper, meeting him in the middle to kiss before un-boarding the plane.

CHAPTER 2:
MORE THAN BROKEN

Let's be honest here. Every group of ladies has a wild card. The one friend who finds it hard to keep her mouth shut. Cusses like a sailor but loves Jesus. The one that is the fiercest but most loyal. You never know what she's gonna say or catch her doin'. It's me! I'm the wild card in my group. If you are just lookin' for some fun or a nice night out, take a gander on me. Jet black hair, dark olive skin, and piercing blue eyes. A face and body most would think I bargained with the devil for. I'm unapologetic and will drink you under the table. My escape is riding my handsome horse in wide open pastures as fast as he can go. Livin does not exist until you feel the wind whip through your hair as you fly across the countryside on a horse you give all control to. For kicks, I dabble with my own, on my own and sometimes multiples. But always in the mood for playing with the opposite. Now let's go have some fun!

"Damnit, Tilly! Did you really post this on the dating app? I think I might murder you myself tonight. Givin' me an excuse not to date because I'll be behind bars!" I yell at her.

"Look! You have been down since lover boy took off to Brazil for the next six months with no promise of keeping his dick in his pants. You said yourself y'all aren't exclusive anymore so have some fun with it. Paramour is under renovations for the next three months so you can change it up some. It won't kill you to try something new."

Tilly is right. I need to be over him. This isn't me. Pining over some guy. Even if he has delicious abs, a smile that melts my heart, and the biggest drilling tool I have ever encountered. I've never been exclusive with anyone, since the other one. Until him. But he damn got himself under my skin with me tryn' to claw him out painfully now. "I hate this feelin', and it's not fair he has me all jacked up over here while he is galavanting over South America doing every hot pussy and ass I'm sure he finds."

"Now let's not jump to conclusions. He's over there for work, and Nash stated he was going to be pretty busy," Willa spits out. More so to protect Nash from any of my scrutiny.

"Quit findin' excuses for why he hasn't texted or called in three weeks!" Blake should be feelin' lucky Willa married into that family as that is serving as his protection from me putting a hit out on him. Poppin' open another Busch light, I lay back on the couch. A whining Hamlet jumps on the couch to lay on top of me. "I'm not givi'n' his dog back," I hiss, making a loud statement to them. Thinking of the last few months together. That he kept pushing to get my heart, and when he finally did, the mother fucker left. He did the exact thing he promised me he would not do. Leave!

"What happened again the last night you saw him?" Tilly asks.

"Why do you always ask me to retell the story?"

"Because we must be missing something. You two were pretty hot and heavy before y'all even disappeared for a month. Then y'all came back, and we're completely inseparable until a few weeks ago. You two even seemed fine when you knew he was heading to Brazil."

"Trust me. I've gone over it a million times in my head already. He's just a spoiled playboy fuck-wad that I need to forget about. What type of human being would stand up their lover the night before they leave the country for six months? He could've called, texted, come over. Hell, airmail would have been nice. A thousand ways to communicate what the hell was goin' on. Instead, he ghosted me. Did he wanna break up? He got his damn wish, if so." My thoughts go back to the night he told me he was leaving for six months.

Flashback:
"Amity, I know this is awful timing, but it's my job, and I need to close these deals."

"I get it, Blake, I do. But you disappearing for six months with no possibility of seeing each other is bullshit." Slamming my laptop down on the table, I groan. "Fuck. I hate this feelin' of being attached and needin' you." His jaw clenches and hands roll into fists.

"What the hell you trying to say?"
"I don't know, Blake. Just be done raising your voice." A small vase off my floating shelf goes flying by me, smashing into a million pieces on the opposite wall of Blake. Him wanting to prove a point that he can get much worse and that I am testing his every nerve. I refuse to cave. "Damn you! I wish I never met you!" I scream out, stomping away toward my room.

"Don't you dare walk away from me, Amity," he growls out. Before I can slam my bedroom door, he catches it with his hand, swinging the door back open. "You're envoking the bear."
"I don't give a rat's ass about your big, bad scary self. I've been through worse. You don't scare me."
"I'm not trying to scare you. Just letting you know I'm about to blow a fucking gasket. Besides, what the hell does that mean? You've been through worse?"
Cussing my own mouth for letting stuff slip, I mutter "Nothing. Forget I said anything." Looking up at him, I sigh. "Look, you do you. I'm going to bed. Stay or don't."
"That's always your damn answer. You shut down and push shit aside like you never said it. Like I am supposed to forget. Just

like in Costa Rica when I had to wake you up from a nightmare, because you were screaming and crying so bad. Or when you wigged out in the market because you thought you saw a ghost from the past. You don't give me much to go on."

"Past is my past, Blake. You have my heart, take or leave it." Ready to stomp off again to not have to face him pressuring me to discuss dreadful memories, he pulls my arm, slamming me into his hard body.

"I took your heart, and I am never giving it back. Never." Sliding his fingers through my hair, he murmurs, "One day maybe I will earn your trust to tell me, but this between us is far from over." Then he smashes his lips to mine, before I can protest. My lust for him consumes my mind and body. Letting him take me from behind against my bedroom wall. Every thrust of his cock and hips earns a moan from me and an explicit followed by how I am his by him. By the time we fell into bed, we had forgiven each other and accepted the future that lay ahead.

Current:

"Yah, the whole thing just seems precarious. All Nash would tell me was that when Blake left the office that Tuesday, he was pretty upset about a few things that were discussed. But, of course, he wouldn't disclose much to me. Which leads me to believe it had something to do with you, Amity, because that's the only time he doesn't tell me something. Only when it has to do with somebody in our circle. He knows I don't keep anything from yall! Nash told me last night that Blake will eventually reach out after he calms down and pulls the bat out of his ass."

"That's what I don't understand. What is he so damn hell-bent about? And if it has something to do with me, be a man and talk to me. Fuck my pineapples! This is why I don't do relationships. I don't do drama, emotions, or bullshit!"

"Oh, you did have that one relationship!"

"Tilly, we do not talk about him. That's null and void."

"I know we don't. But that was a turning point for you. You have been a Spitfire from hell water since the day I met you. But he broke something inside of you that you've never fully come back from. At least not until Blake." I refrain from speaking.

Willa speaks up. "What Tilly is trying to say is we love you. We just noticed how happier you've been since Blake has been around since before. Not say'n that you were not happy prior to him. Just seemed like something was missing for you. And you were just trying to fulfill it with all these people and bedroom activities. Using them before they could use you."

"Yah, well I promised myself I would never be taken advantage of again. I gave in to a little happiness and broke my own damn promise. It's unforgivable. I can never forgive him. I have sulked and cried for weeks now." I breathe a weak sigh. "Y'all, I don't cry over nothin'. It's like having an outer body experience. I'm watchin' myself fall apart daily all while trying to tell myself to get my shit together and move on! Now it's time. Time to get back on the saddle and move on."

They give me their best understanding smiles. "I'll be fine y'all. I have a cute apartment, I have a great job, I have the best friends in the world, and now a great dog. I'm good."

Looking around, the living room still houses pictures of Blake and I. Pictures he got printed and framed from our trip to surprise me with before he left. How do two people go from being inevitably enthralled with each other to ashes? I can tell my best friends that I am fine, but deep down, I know I'm not. Not at least for a long haul. I miss him. He became a constant in my life, and I felt genuinely cared for and that he wanted to be here with me. I felt safe. I miss the laughs and the never-ending banter between us. Blake got me on some whole other level that no one ever has. We could make stupid jokes while having intellectual conversations in the same breath. I miss his wit. His touch. His embrace. Every time I walk in my bedroom, I get a whiff of his Juniper smell, pulling me into a daydream.

I scrub my hands across my face.

"Are we goin' out tonight? Or just going to sit here and whine like a bunch of hopeless ninnies?" Tilly and Willa go into a giggle fit, only annoying me more.

When I get up to throw my beer can away, Willa shouts across the room, "Yes, let's go. It's Thirsty Thursday at *Howl*."

With that I change into my hot, tight black leather pants, red cropped halter top, leaving my hair down and wavy. Tilly does my smokey eye makeup as Willa calls Lana, giving her twenty to get herself ready. Final touch, *I'm not paying for shit* red lipstick.

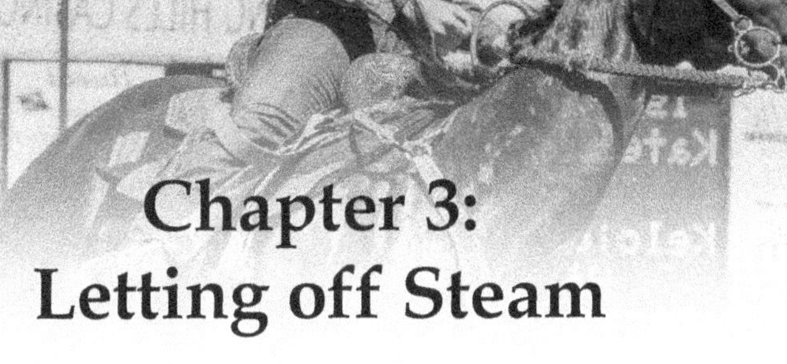

Chapter 3:
Letting off Steam

An hour and a half later, we pull up to *Howl*. All of us hot ladies are ready to party it up. With Willa married, I will have to lean on the other two to be my wingmen tonight. Like literally. Though I suspect Tilly has something going on with Willa's brother, Dirks. She denies the possibility every time I ask, which is probably every other week. I'm going to catch them one day in the barn humping each other in the hay. I just know it.

That might just leave me with sweet, beautiful Lana. Still recovering from a broken heart when we learned her perfect relationship and her perfect life was not so grand. Short story, he pushed for her to quit her job to stay at home. Not because the man makes hundreds of thousands of dollars and they could afford her not working, but because he wanted to come home to a clean house, laundry done, and dinner cooked every night. Be a trophy wife he kept in a glass case. He started even keeping her from seeing us. We suspected something was up, but it was when we caught him out at Paramour, everything came to a head. First, we thought he was just entertaining a few clients. Then Tilly saw him entertaining another woman's cunt in the lady's restroom stall. He walked out, and I was there waiting for him. Punched him so hard, I knocked him on his ass, giving him a black eye. *Still pissed off at the whole scene.* He was unapologetic and not worried we caught him. More like irate we ruined his good time. Telling us Lana would pay for embarrassing him. Still not sure what that meant, because the next day, Lana took off to Fort Worth for two months to stay with her parents. All before coming back home and moving in with Tilly. She's been pretty quiet ever since.

Heading to the bar, we take our usual seats and order a round of whiskey shots to get the night goin'. It's not until ten when the crowd finally picks up. More eye candy to view. Around eleven, Nash shows up with Clint after a business dinner they had over at Bohanans. Only reminding me that the lone-wolf Blake is still MIA. Nash takes Willa out to the dance floor, while Tilly and Clint follow. Looking over at Lana, I shrug a shoulder. "Me and you babe, come on." I drag her out to dance. This blonde beauty in front of me needs a break, I spot Jake from one of my group night stands and wave him over to us. "Jake, you remember Lana, right?"

"Of course, how could I forget the voluptuous blonde goddess." She blushes, and I love it.

"You know she is no longer taken, so if you would like to dance with her, you are free to do so." He quickly takes her hand and twirls her around the dance floor. I see the flash of smile we have all missed so much. *See I am a nice person. I just have to like you.* Turning around quickly, I run into a pair of boobs. "Well long time no see, Am."

Kissing each other's cheeks, I pull her into a quick hug. "Hey Cami."

"Where's your puppy dog tonight?"

"Excuse me?"

"You know the dirty blonde hot piece of ass that is usually with you. The one I enjoyed with you forever ago."

Trying to hide my disgust at the mention of him, I mutter, "Blake you mean. Yah, he is traveling for work right now."

Excitement flashes through her dark brown eyes, bringing her hand to run down the side of my arm. "Does that mean you are free?"

Letting out a loose laugh, I smile. "I am, Cami, what do you have in mind?"

"Lots," she giggles, dragging me to the dance floor. "But first we are going to dance our hearts out for a while." Cami is gorgeous with her long brown hair, pristine complexion on a flawless face, wide eyes, and refined nose. Perky breasts and a killer body with all the curves. We dance and grind, then go for more shots.

One in the morning, and this place is still rocking. A plethora of shots and drinks in, we are all going to be hurting tomorrow. Thankfully it's summer and no Friday classes for me. Out on the dance floor again, I am sandwiched between Cami and some hot guy named Carter. I'm pretty sure he is the Calvin Klein model that graces my view on the billboard as I head in to work everyday. My ass is grinding against his crotch while Cami rubs up against my front. Both their hands slipping up my bare stomach and under my crop top. I lean my head back on Carter's shoulder as he gropes my breasts. Cami is kissing my bare stomach now. *I need this.* I have missed being touched sexually. Really being touched at all. This feels sublime. Hands and lips all over me, to be wanted by someone. Like I'm the oxygen to their lungs. I pull Cami up and take her mouth with mine. Placing my hand between her legs, rubbing against her heat, as I continue to grind against Carter. He begins kissing my neck, and I am ready to explode right in the middle of the dance floor.

"We need to go," I whisper to both of them. They nod in agreement. "Let me tell my friends." I head over to the crew, thinking all seem five sheets to the wind. *I'm one to talk!*

Tilly runs up to me and gives me a hug. "Look at you breaking the dry spell. Fuck, that was hot!"

"You're always welcome to join, Til." She giggles and takes a swig of her water.

Willa hands me a water bottle. "You sure, Am? I just don't want you to act on a moment you may regret."

"I'm good, Wil. He's gone with all promises broken. I need this."

"Okay then. Call me in the morning." Hugging her, I turn to Lana, who is slow dancing with Jake. I blow her a kiss to not interrupt and head out to meet my conquests for the night.

I wake up in the morning to my phone buzzing off the chain. Slowly adjusting to my bearings, I realize I am at Cami's house. Sandwiched between her and Carter from last night. I reach over him to turn my phone off, but before I do, I see a text from Blake.

Nope, not dealing with that bullshit today. OFF.

I slightly jump when I feel Carter's teeth on my nipple, then he sucks, causing me to moan in pleasure. "Good morning to you too," I coo, leaning down to kiss him. His hands roam up my body, caressing my skin. Kissing each other with such heat, I'm wet instantly. I reach under the covers to begin stroking his cock in my hand. Finding him well and hard to go. I move over top of him, sliding my center down his shaft. Both of us are moaning in pleasure. I lift up and slowly slide down him a few times, teasing and taunting him with my body. Caressing my own breasts. "You are too much, Amity."

"Don't forget it." I slam down on him fast this time, taking him deep to ride him hard like a bull. Pushing him to the edge while circling my clit with my fingers. We wake Cami, who wakes up gorgeous as always, and crawls over and kisses Carter while he fondles her breasts. I ride him until he releases himself with a loud groan into Cami's mouth. I managed to hold myself out.

Pain and Pleasure. How long can I push myself to last before it's so painful I need a release?

Lifting my body off Carter, I slide down and take him in my mouth. "You taste divine mixed in with me." I moan around his head, then pop my mouth off him.

"Oh, I need to taste this, roll over, peaches, I need you." I do as Cami says, as she kisses her way down my body. Caleb lays next to us enjoying his view, building himself up for the next round. Cami kisses my center and uses her delicate tongue to slice through my folds. Her moans let me know she agrees how we taste together, and I watch her finger herself into an orgasm while she feasts on me. Then I kiss Carter, pulling on Cami's hair as she pushes us both over the edge. Carter flips Cami over to lick her up, then pushes his shaft into her. Watching their beautiful bodies mold together, trying not to think of who I wish was with me right now. Who would love being in the middle but ensuring he would be the only one bringing me to the edge. Escorting me to my peak.

"Let me taste you now, peaches." He flips himself and Cami over, so she is riding him now, as I place my cunt right over his mouth. "Fuck yeah," he speaks out. I hold onto the headboard of the bed as he pushes his fingers into me and laps me up. I hold my release in, wanting to ride him again. Cami and I switch places but not before a mini make out session over Carter where he drives his fingers into us. Once I am straddling him again and Cami is on his face, I go to town. Letting all my ambitions go, letting myself free from the pain. I peak over my cusp and ride my high down slowly as he pulses inside my core.

CHAPTER 4:
UNKNOWN NUMBER

I turn my phone back on when I walk into my apartment. Luckily I saw a note on my door that Lana had stopped by last night to grab Hamlet. I will have to get her nightly scoop later, but right now I need a shower and food before I can deal with a text message from Blake. I take a quick shower, though, scrubbing my skin red and raw. I'm not quite sure how I feel about last night or this morning.

Was it fun? Yes.

Was it sexy and erotic? Of course.

Was it Blake? No.

Before I met him that scenario would be a weekly thing for me. Even after we started being with each other, that was at least one to two times a month. Then halfway through our Costa Rica trip, we became exclusive. Just him and me. Two people who never thought love was in the cards for them because of their nature and personalities found love under the endless starry sky beyond the rainforest. Not even sure words were spoken, but he took my heart. *I want my fucking heart back.*

I slowly dry off to get dressed. Then I take my time walking to the kitchen and grabbing a parfait from the fridge, before sitting at the table with my phone in my hand. Tapping the screen, I see four missed calls from Willa, one from Tilly, and a million messages from both of them. Still ignoring Blake's text message, I call Willa.

"Oh my Hades, please tell me you are alive, and this is not someone pretending to be you?"

"Jesus, pineapples, Wil, it's me. Alive and well. What the hell is going on?"

"Hmph. Maybe you should check your text messages and call your best friends back."

"That is what I am doing now."

"Whatever. Any who… Did you hear from Blake by any chance?"

"He messaged me, but I have yet to check it."

"Ummmm okay. Don't panic, but Clint's drunk ass sent a picture to him last night with your dance floor threesome." She spits this out so fast I barely catch all the words.

In my mind, I am thinking I am going to kick Clint's ass, but the bad bitch in me says, "who cares. Remember, Blake didn't just leave, he disappeared. I could care less what he saw."

"Well, he called Nash this morning, losing his shit about the picture. Giving him Hades about how he and Clint were supposed to be watching over you, keeping you out of trouble. That it's all Nash's fault he lost you, and he is depressed in Brazil." I soak in what Willa is saying. *Depressed in Brazil? Why would he blame Nash?*

She continues, "I'm trying to get it out of Nash what happened, but he is being an ass hat because he knows I'll run to you with the information. I'll keep wearing him down, but check your message from Blake and check in with me later, okay? I have to head to the ranch for lessons this morning."

"Alright. Thanks, Be safe." First, I go change Blake's name in my contacts, then I look at his text, wondering how I should respond.

Tool: What the duck! Is this how you show your love for someone? As soon as they leave, you hook up with other people?

ME: Sorry, I don't know a duck. *Clearly knowing he meant the other word.*
Nice to hear from you! If it wasn't for Nash, I might've thought your plane crashed in the Gulf.
Tool: Don't start with me, woman! I'm at a client lunch or I would call and cuss you out right now.
ME: You could try, but I wouldn't answer. Have a nice life, Blake.
Tool: Dammit! You are mine, Amity. You are to be with no one else until I get back. MINE!
ME: Please ship my heart back via next day air. It called and said it's ready to move on.
Tool: Don't poke the bear, Princess! It won't end well.
ME: I can poke the bear all I want. He's not here to stop me. As far as I'm concerned, he left and disappeared for three weeks. So the bear can go fuck himself and call somebody who cares.

Phone starts to ring. Ignore. Then I block his number.

Five minutes go by and a text from Willa comes in.

Willa: Did you block Blake?
ME: Yep!
Willa: Zeus' balls, Amity!
ME: Let me screenshot this conversation for you.
Pic sent
....
Willa: That son of a bitch! What is his endgame?
ME: Not sure I care anymore.
Willa: Please hold, Nash is calling me.

I go about finishing my parfait, clean up the kitchen and start laundry, waiting for Willa to get back to me. An hour later, my phone buzzes with a message from an unknown number.

Unknown: You can't ignore me, Princess?

ME: Who the fuck is this?

Unknown: You know damn well who this is!

ME: Who's phone are you texting me from?

Unknown: Don't worry about it, just know you poked the bear.

ME: OK. Blocking this number too. Bye!

Buzz…oh good… This is actually Willa.

Willa: Sorry… Some of the cows got out. We had to wrangle them up. Nash was losing his shit because you blocked Blake.

ME: God for bid! Tell Nash to get his panties out of a wad.

Willa: Amity!

ME: You know it's true. Besides, the asshole just texted me from another number.

Willa: Maybe you should just hear him out.

ME: No, I think I'm good.

ME: Look, I need to go pick up Hamlet from Lana and get stuff done around the house before I'm at the ranch all day tomorrow.

Willa: OK, well keep me posted.

My phone buzzes again with another number.
That shithead! I go to open it.

Unknown: I have my reasons.

ME: OK.   *Changing name in phone*

Asshat: You're going to listen to them.

ME: No, I don't think I will.

Asshat: Are we having our first real fight?

ME: If that makes you feel better about the situation, sure.

ME: Don't you have clients to wine and dine?

Asshat: Yes. I'm multitasking.

ME: Who's phone this time?

Asshat: My assistant.

ME: Oh, is she cute?

Asshat: Yes. Ross is super cute.

Pic downloading

I am greeted with the polar opposite of Blake. Short, balding, slightly overweight, some weird long goatee thing happening of a Ross.

ME: Wow! You must be experimenting.

Asshat: Fuck you, Amity!

ME: You only wish you could.

Asshat: That's true.

ME: I really need to go do stuff. Do I need to block this number too?

Asshat: No, but can you unblock mine.

ME: No.

ME: Maybe I'll see you when you get back in five months.

Asshat: You counting down the days?

ME: No. I ripped up our calendar and let Hamlet pee on it. *I didn't actually, but he doesn't need to know otherwise.*

Asshat: Wtf!

ME: Bye, Asshat.

Phone off.

Pushing down my thoughts of what just played out, I leave to head to Lana and Tilly's to pick up Hamlet. Walking into their place, I throw myself on their couch. They are both at the kitchen table eating sandwiches with Hamlet begging for a bite.

"Boy trouble?" Tilly asks.

"You could say that. But I know you both know the story already. So let's not rehash it."

BLAKE

Back in my suite, I have already thrown the whole bar to the floor. Except the one glass I saved to still be able to drink. I need a fucking drink, but nothing is strong enough to push the sick feeling of letting her down. The knot-churning ache that I pissed my girl off. That there is no forgiveness on the table. The feeling I have been fighting since I stepped on that plane and left without a word. Amity sees me now like everyone else always has. *Spoiled rich playboy.* I have no real reason to act the way I do. I just really enjoy people and sex. All forms. Never been in a relationship to know my emotional capacity. Never cared to learn someone enough to care about their feelings. Never had to answer to anyone other than myself and family at times. Never thought I could become infatuated with one person. Never, until Amity.

A few days after the announcement I was headed to South America to oversee phase two of a project, I went to Nash and Clint. Told them I wanted to propose to Amity before I took off. Giving her a promise that I was fully committed to her, to us.

Brother Nash and Clint were elated for me. Businessmen Clint and Nash reminded me of the protocols. Our investigator must dig up all the dirt before entering that kind of commitment. I'm a Holdings. Worth millions of dollars with a large company at stake. My parents and family love Amity with all her brashness and beauty.

Regardless, we have to secure our assets and name. To gain the knowledge of secrets before some sleazy reporter does. Nash did the same thing with Willa. Though she is an open book with a spotless record. Amity on the other hand, has not always been forthcoming with information. She prefers to focus on the now, over dwelingl on the past.

Only from Nash and Willa do I know Amity's dad was a washed-up rodeo circuit alcoholic. Not a nice one either by the stories Nash shared with me in confidence, because Willa would sever his balls if she knew he overshared. Amity's mom eventually removed them from the situation and remarried another cowboy. That's what brought them to San Antonio. She calls him dad and seems like a good guy. Though not always offered a fair hand in life. The ranch has struggled on and off for years, almost keeping Amity from finishing college. They seem afloat now, but a secret grant might have been given to certain ranches that met certain criteria. Only Willa and Amity's ranches qualified. A secret Nash and I will take to our graves.

Flashbacks of the time we have spent together since day two cause the hair on my arms to rise. From all the times I could tell she was pushing me away when I got too close. Not because she didn't want me, but because something internally was holding her back. All the times I would awaken to her having nightmares, tossing and turning, murmuring and screaming names, and to get away from her. The scars she has on her hips that she passes off as stretch marks. I have been with enough women in my life to know what actual stretch marks look like, and these are clearly faded scars. The first time I noticed them was when I was determined to learn every inch of her body with my mouth. I remember her whole body tensing when my lips met her skin over the scars. I had looked up at her, but her face stayed stone as she stared at the ceiling. It was not the time or place to ask questions, nor were we that close then for me to be invasive. She has loosened up over time about them, but I still feel a slight tense when my fingers or lips glide over the markings.

Amity has sent me into rants when she would spew words about not fearing me or she has already been through hell and back, with no explanation whatsoever. Without Nash sharing the information he knew; I would be completely in the dark about her past. It took months for Amity to accept me for more than a roll in the sheets. She proved to me I had met my match, and I have wanted no one else since. Her heart is like mine, and I plan to keep her.

Needless to say, when I was handed the file on Amity Jean Mercer the day before I was leaving, shock was an understatement. Nash did not hold any of the information in the file against Amity but was hell bent on getting answers before I went over there that night to ask the only question I wanted an answer to. She had a past, an interesting one. I have re-read those pages, each time thinking I was reading some outdated medieval story. The last thing I wanted to do was dredge up the past with her right before leaving. I had no wiggle room with my schedule to even try to delay for a day or two. *Fuck!* I tell myself daily I'm a fucking moron for leaving or not reaching out to her. Now she has moved on.

All I have done is jerk off in my hand to memories of her for the past three weeks. While she is out having a threesome and probably more. My brothers told me it was the first time she had been out in weeks, to not suspect any other foul play had happened. How can I not? I broke her. She legit asked for her heart back. Picking up my phone, I call Nash. I need to get home, even for just a couple of days.

"Hey, brother. She un-block you yet?" he asks, but I'm barely able to hear him because his background is loud.

"No, asshole. Where the hell are you?" He flips to facetime. Seven o'clock on Friday, and they are at the karaoke bar.

"Stay on, your girl is about to perform." Grinning from ear to ear, I ache to catch a glance of her and listen to her sing. I miss hearing her voice carry through the apartment. She reminds me of an old soul with a raspy voice like Patsy Cline. Typically, that is who she is singing or Reba. I watch her take the stage, laughing with her head tilted back a little. I miss her beautiful laugh, how the dimple in her right cheek presses in. How her luscious top lip curls up when she brings her mouth into a genuine smile. My eyes swipe her head to toe through the screen. She looks so edible, and I become more angry I am not there with her. That she is looking like a temptation in cowboy boots and a short fitted dress, outlining her breasts in perfect form down to her divine sultry curves. I hear all our friends shouting her name and cheering her on when the music starts up.

"Crazy. I'm crazy for feeling so lonely. I'm crazy. I'm crazy for feelin' so blue. I knew, you'd love me as long as you wanted. And then someday, you'd leave me for somebody new."

I watch her close her eyes while she sways to the music, knowing she is feeling every beat and word in her bones. Her voice carrying on like an alluring siren.

Drawing everyone in to feel her heart. To feel her pain. I'm memorized and near tears knowing it was me that caused her suffering. Near the end of the song, she looks back toward her crew and realizes I'm on the other side of the screen. Locking eyes with me, singing the last verse directly toward me. "Crazy for thinking my love could hold you. I'm crazy for tryin'. And crazy for cryin'. And I'm crazy for lov'n you." The crowd erupts for her as they always do. I decide to end the call, booking the next flight home.

CHAPTER 5: RANCH DAY

"Tilly. That little shit over there won't stop harassing the cows. Can you go deal with him before I rope'em up and throw him into the trough." She looks over to the kid then back to me laughing.

"Amity, he is like five."

"Pineapples! I don't care. He's getti'n them all riled up and antsy. We are moving them tomorrow, so I'd prefer a calm herd."

"I'll deal with him." Tilly heads over to get the kid while I tack up Nevada.

I rode Henry this morning on the trail ride since we had a few elderly people on the sunrise tour this morning. Felt best to take the ride steady and slow. Now I am going to kick my day up a notch by high-tailing the landscape with Nevada. With us not competing in reining until the season starts back in January along with ropin', I try to get him out for exercise several times a week. Whether we are runnin' through the pastures or working on patterns. "Look at you all cleaned up. Now if you would just stop rolling around on the ground after rain showers, we'd be good." Patting him on the side, he neighs in response. I've shined up his white patches and glossed the black on his overo coat, then brushed his mane and saddled up. Exiting the cross-ties, Dirks walks in.

"Have you seen Tilly?"

"She is kickin' some kid's ass for me. Why, she late for a hookup?" He shakes his head at me.

"No Amity. She was going to help Willa and me train the new filly, but I need to go help Pa pack up for the cattle drive tomorrow. Ben went home early because his kid is sick."

"Oh, well you always seem to have a reason for her. Need my help?" I waggle my eyebrows, giving him my devilish grin, causing him to chuckle.

"Nah, we will deal with the filly next week. She's out in the north pasture if you want to go check on her though. She's rugged and wild."

"I bet she just needs some tough love. But yeah, I'll ride Nevada over there before we head out."

"Thanks. See yah."

"See yah," I murmur, then head out, riding Nevada up a dirt path to the north pasture. "Good boy," I say to him as he trots along.

We are gone for what seems hours by the time we make it back to the barn. Untacking Nevada, I brush him down, talking to him. "You are the best boy. The only guy I need in my life, huh?" He nudges me with his big white nose.

"Doc clearly has some competition," Willa says, coming down the pathway with Doc Holiday walking behind her.

I laugh, "He does. Y'all just get done?"

"Yep. Ranch is packed for the next few weeks. I guess everyone is tryin' to get in last minute vacations before school starts back up. We had twelve kids alone today in basic training class. I'm actually looking forward to the cattle drive tomorrow to just be able to ride."

"How many folks have signed up for that?"

"Tilly told me ten. We do try to limit the people, because we would be losing more riders than cows out there. I know people come from all over for the experience, but they don't realize how rough the terrain is out there let alone keeping up with the herd. We have six calves right now. I told Pa I would prefer to wrangle them up and trailer them over to the new spot. He told me that would take away the fun and experience. So then I told him he will be chasin' them down."

"You know damn well it will be us ropin' them up."

"Ugh, I know." We both laugh hard, and the release of emotions feels almost imposing to how I've felt these last several weeks. Willa and I both walk our horses down to the east pasture to release them.

"I checked on that new filly today. Gotta name for her yet?"

"How was she? She's going to be a challenge to break. I can tell. Um, the last owner called her Larken."

"That is fitting. The black that runs down her muzzle and legs makes her look fierce. She is a beautiful Dun."

"She is. I'm hoping to get some time in with her before school starts back up. I would love to introduce her to the rodeo program at school. We have two horses retiring this year and need to start looking for replacements."

"Let me talk to old man Woodrow next week. He has several paints and a mustang over there he got in a few months back. I'm sure if you felt they were worthy, he would work out a deal with you. He lets me use his ranch for field trips when my students need hands-on agriculture experience. Plus, his wife makes and sells the best peach cobbler ice cream this side of the state."

"Mmmm, now you have me craving peach cobbler. Damn. Can I go with you next week?"

"Of course. I'll call him Monday and see what works for him."

"Thanks, Am. Well, let's get home to rest. Long day tomorrow." We hug and head to our trucks.

Exhausted, I walk into my apartment greeted with a jovial Hamlet. "Sorry, boy, I know it was a long day for you. Did Lana come and play with you?" Squishing his face together, I baby-talk him because he has the most adorable, fluffy, squishy face ever. "You're too handsome for your own good, Ham. Come on. Let's go make dinner."

I begin grilling some chicken in a pan with a side of rice and green beans. As all of that is cooking, I pull out the ingredients to make a salad to put my chicken on. Hamlet starts sniffing and barking at the door. "What is it boy?" I walk over, looking through the peephole. "No one's there. Stop your babbling." He begins to follow me back to the kitchen, but then stops in his tracks and heads back to the door. "Whatever," I whisper under my breath, going back to making my salad.

Knock, Knock.

"Pineapples, I don't want visitors tonight." Checking my phone, I have no messages from anyone stating they were coming over. Looking through the peephole again, no one. Hamlet is whining so I open the door to show him nobody was out there, yet he flies out the door to the left. Running out to chase him, I'm taken back by who I see. "Hamlet get inside now!" I say angrily. He chooses to ignore me with the return of our guest. "Fine, be a traitor," I grumble, walking into my apartment and slamming the door.

Knock, Knock.

I ignore the sound, taking the chicken off the skillet and draining the macaroni before stirring the cheese in.

Knock, knock, knock. Bark, bark, knock, knock, bark.

Jesus those two. Stomping over, I fling the door open. "Do you need to be excessively annoying?"

"He's hungry. It smells amazing."

"Hamlet, get in here. Go away, Blake." He pads in and sits behind me. I try to slam the door, but Blake's shoe catches the door before it slams. "Please, Amity. I traveled all this way to see you."

"Wow, I feel so honored." Turning away, I ignore him, knowing he just walked in, shut the door, and is making his way to me in the kitchen. "Are you hungry?"

"I am, but don't worry about me." Like old habits, I make him a plate with extra rice with butter. I set our plates down at the table and put Hamlet's on his mat to eat.

Blake hesitates before picking up his fork. "I didn't poison it if that's what you're thinkin'."

He chuckles, "I would understand if you did."

"I'm glad we can agree on something." We lock eyes, and it takes every fiber of my being to look away. My core is yearning for him. My heart is beating rapidly for him. My skin is tingling with the want to touch and be touched by him. I force myself to eat, though, I've lost all appetite since he arrived, but I know I need fuel for tomorrow. Silence passes for several minutes. I can fill my eyes twitching with the anxiety that I'm beginning to feel. More silence with him casting glances my way. Dropping my fork loudly on the plate, I ask, "What are you doing here, Blake?"

"Isn't it obvious? I came to see you."

"Your timing is impeccable!" I snap back.

"Can you stop being such a bitch for ten minutes and hear me out?"

"Honestly, no," I say with a smirk, getting up from my chair and walking in the kitchen to clear my dishes. Not as soon as I set them on the counter, he has my wrists in his hands, pinning me to the fridge. I know he would never hurt me so it's not fear that rushes through me. Only anger that he thinks he can come into my home and expect something from me.

He growls out, "The bear is here, Amity. What are you going to do now?"

"Let you have your temper tantrum, and then hopefully you'll leave." Slamming his fist into the fridge above my head, keeping my wrist held in his other large hand.

"Dammit, woman. You're making me crazy. Pushing my limits."

"This is good, Blake. You're learning where your limits are. You're learning what raw anger and heartbreak feel like," I grind out through gritted teeth.

"My heart is not breaking, Princess. I'm not letting you go."

"Ha! What's done is done, Blake. Please just leave."

"You are so fucking stubborn. You know you want me! You know you love me! But you are so damn stubborn to hear me out. To give us a chance."

"YOU want a chance? You left me!" I spit out. He releases my wrists and walks away, running his hand through his hair and down his face, pacing.

"I know! I fucked up. Trust me, I've been agonizing over all this." He's back in my space again, towering over me. Toe to toe. His face leaning down to me, I can feel him breathing in the scent of my hair. Both of us are near in pants with anger and exhilarated emotions running through our veins. Blake plants his hands on the fridge above my head, leaning closer in. "Amity, just look at me, please."

Against my better judgment, I do. His baby blues pierce my own with anguish. A quick thought flashes through my mind. *What if? What if I have him one more time?*

It's what he wants anyhow. Then we can both go our separate ways. I grab a fistful of his shirt, pulling him down to my level and kiss him. He backs away from me confused. Pulling my shirt over my head, standing there in my pink laced bra and jeans, I ask, "Isn't this what you want?" stepping toward him and trapping him between the counter and my body.

"I do, but not like this."

"This is all you get, Blake, take me or leave." I begin to walk away. He lets me get farther than I thought he would before he pushes me down on the couch.

"You will be the death of me, Amity. Tell me your mine." Staying silent, I stare back at him, unaffected. "Maybe you need a reminder of what you've been missing."

I slip a sly smile, egging him on. I won't deny my body this, but my heart is going to stay out of this moment. He slips out of his clothes, leaving just his briefs on. His bulge is on full display. My eyes wander over the body I've yearned for. The muscular arms I ache to hold me. Blake quickly jerks my panties off with my jeans and unclasps my bra from the back. He's moving with vigor, pulling me to the floor beneath him. Without warning or foreplay, he pushes his way in. My mind is fighting my body's needs to have him. He rails me deep with rapid thrusts.

"Harder," I grit out. I want him to tear me apart so I can feel any other pain but heartache. His arm slips under my lower back side, pulling my bottom half up closer to him. I claw and rake my nails up and down his back and neck. Gripping his hair in my fingers. "Harder, Blake." In a swoop of motion, he pulls out, flips my front over the couch to take me from behind. He slides in, then wraps my hair around his fist. Holding me down on my lower back with his palm as he tightens his grip on my hair, slamming into me with all his strength. My legs are turning to jell-o trying to hold up against the couch. I moan in response to my inner core enjoying his cock savaging my heat repeatedly. We both reach out releases together, leaving him panting over me, pressing me further into the cushion. Once he moves, I take my chance to stand up to dress myself. I'm as far as bra and panties when he grabs my arm, turning me around to face him.

SLAP!

Tears fall like heavy rain down my cheeks. He holds his cheek while I ignore the sting in my palm. "You need to leave, now."

"What? What the hell, Amity? After what we just did?"

"What we just did is I let you fuck me one more time. I have tried for weeks to banish your memory with no avail. You haunt me day and night. Give me my heart back. That's all I am asking of you."

BLAKE

My girl is breaking right in front of me, and I am at a loss. She is begging for her heart back, but is it fair she gets to keep mine if I return hers? "I can't, Amity. My heart doesn't beat without yours. My soul screams without you near. Don't ask me to leave you."

Amity collapses to the ground. I catch her as I guide us carefully down to our knees. Holding her tightly, I rock us back and forth. Her hands are fisted in my shirt. I situate myself to be more comfortable against the couch. Squeezing her to me, letting her know it's not an invitation to move away. "I'll never let you go, Am. It's not in my nature to do nor do I want to. We need to talk, but I won't push the subject tonight. Right now, I just need you to know I love you."

She lets out a shudder with a heavy sob. I continue to rock her for what seems like hours. The best hours I have had in weeks with my girl in my arms. "Amity," I whisper in her ear, noticing her breathing has become steady. A sign she's asleep. Carrying her to bed, I tuck her under the covers with Hamlet laying down by her side. "You look after her tonight, big guy. You hear me?" Petting his head, he whines a little in acknowledgement. Placing her phone on the nightstand to charge. *God, she is the worst about having a charged phone.* Laughing to myself all the times she's had a dead phone when I would try to call. Always in panic, but always had an inkling she would be at the ranch. I'd pull up to her hauling ass across the field on her horse without a care in the world. *Huh!* Amity is not a woman that needs anyone. She chooses who graces her life. How do I convince her I need her? I'm not scared to admit I'm desperate for her love. For her respect. For the way she used to look at me with fire in her eyes. Tonight, all she gave me were ice daggers as I ravishly had my way with her. Giving her all the anger, she wanted behind the act. Then I saw her weakness. *Me.* Walking out of the apartment, I head over to Nash and Willa's to game plan.

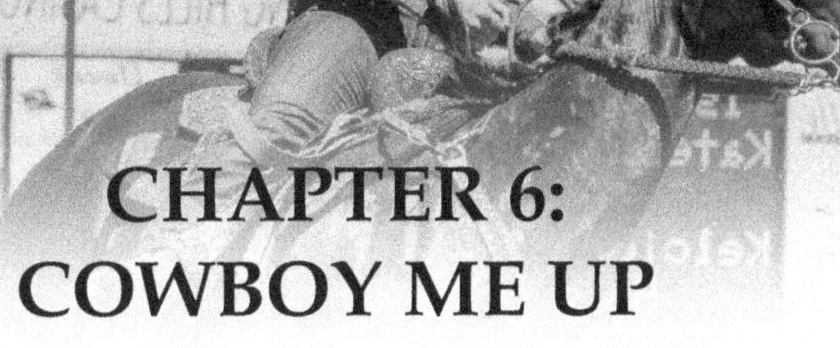

CHAPTER 6:
COWBOY ME UP

The blaring alarm on my phone has me shooting out of the bed. *Damn, three thirty in the morning already?* Stretching, last night beams into my mind. *O Jesus, where is Blake?* I fly out of bed, sprinting into the living room expecting to find him on the couch. Disappointment sets in when I realize it's just Hamlet and me. Just like it has been. I slip on shorts and a sweatshirt then push my feet into my boots. "Come on, boy, lets go outside." Clipping his leash on, we head down the hallway to the elevator. My mind is evaded with the events of last night. Taking a deep breath, we step out into the humid summer morning.

"Hey." I hear.

Turning around, I smile. "Hey, Lana. Of course, you're running on time."

Laughing, she returns my smile, though it almost looks like a grimace. "Love, you look like shit."

"Hmph. Much appreciated, bestie."

"I'll come up with you so you can tell me all about it, then will take Hamlet when you leave."

"Okay, but a lot happened, and I only have twenty minutes, so let's go."

Back in the apartment, I relive every detail with Lana. Watching her facials go from excitement to shock and livid to happiness.

"He's trying, Amity. At least hear him out. It could be anything."

"Right!" Thinking in my head, I ask," Do you think he knows about him?"

"How would he know, Am? He would have to dig really deep to find anything."

"True. If so, it's no excuse for the damage he's inflicted on me. I just know last night with him being here as much as I fought him, every fiber of my soul and body felt content. That I am supposed to be with him. But he ruined all of it."

"How long is he in town for?" she asks.

"He didn't say. I can't imagine long." Folding my hair in a long braid down the back, I go to put my boots on and get ready to walk out.

Lana speaks up, "Just go do your thing today and focus on the task ahead. We are supposed to get some rough weather later this afternoon."

"I do love a good rainstorm while trying to herd cattle across rivers and hills. Something so traditional and hard-core. An exhilarating rush of adrenaline."

"You go have fun in the rain. I will be staying nice and dry with Hamlet."

"Ha, I will. It will be a nice distraction." Tossing her Hamlet's leash, she hooks him up, and we walk out to our vehicles. She gives me a tight squeeze before I step up in my truck.

"Y'all be safe today and send me pictures when you can."

"You mean like the one of Nash trying to be a cowboy and tackling cows or when he tried to take a nap and the calf peed on him?" Laughing, I remember the first time Nash joined us on a cattle drive.

"Exactly!"

Pulling up the gravel road to the ranch, I spot Willa's old beat-up truck parked by the barn. I love her even more for it because Nash got her a brand new loaded-out Chevy truck. Which she loves, but she always prefers to drive her old one. It drives him crazy because it's always breaking down and feels it's not safe anymore. I see Dirks, Nash, and Willa leading the horses and setting out tack. Tilly is already in the zone saddling up horses. I spot someone under the dim lamp post. A guy leaning up against the truck I don't recognize. Walking up to the barn, I step closer to the guy just to get a better view under the lamp post. I easily spot the expensive brand-new boots and tight wranglers under the light, with his head down, looking at his phone. He must be a guest joining us today, and I'm sure I will only be laughing when his feet are killing him an hour into the drive. Shaking my head as this made-up cowboy, I decide to not linger any longer and get my horse ready.

"You not even gonna say good mornin', darlin'?" Thrown off by the words with accent but distinctly recognize the voice, I whip around to be face-to-face with Blake, handing me a coffee. *Fuck me with pineapples this moring*, I think in my head. I take it because I need the caffeine.

"What are you doin' here?"

"Came to spend time with you?"

Taking a deep breath, I ask the million dollar question. "Why?

"Amity, it's really early, and I haven't slept. I am here to spend time with you. Hopefully get you to listen to me in the middle of all the chaos today."

"Not stoppin' you from joining today, Blake, but I'm not goin' to be doin' any favors for you either."

"I know what I'm doing out there"

"You have never once done a cattle drive. It's not all fun and games plus we're getting a storm later."

"I watched YouTube last night. And that show, *Yellowstone*. Gave me perspective."

"Jesus. Take the reins now," I breathe out. Spotting Nash and Willa walking into the barn, I yell, "Nash, come get your brother!"

"No can-do, Am. He is all yours." Blake turns back and grins at me. I look at him with disgust even though the inner me is pleased.

"Okay, boss, I'm all yours. Put me to work."

Sighing, I shake my head. "You first need to go get your horse tacked up. And I hope you packed lunch and a thermos and water."

"Already tacked up and ready to go, boss. And Willa made sure I have all that packed this morning."

"Oh. Did she now?" Looking over my shoulder, I find her grinning ear to ear at me, only for me to salute her with my middle finger.

"Can I help you?" he endearingly asks.

"Sure. You can go grab my saddle pack and hat out of the cab of my truck."

"On it," he says, as he struts away in his painted-on Wranglers that makes his ass look edible. I get Nevada tacked up and help with the rest of the horses for the guests.

At five the guests start arriving and Dirks starts going over the rules and expectations of the day.

"I am your trail boss for today. Meaning, I will be upfront of you and the herd with Pa."

Willa tosses me a lunch sack from the kitchen, and I whisper, "Thank you," during Dirks' speech. She knows I always make sure everyone else is well prepared but then forget my own shit. I'm pretty much tuning out the rest of the speech because it's not nothin' I haven't heard before. And I know my spot as a swing.

Finally Dirks finishes and starts barking orders of placement. I mount Nevada in preparation to head out. Tilly leans over next to me. "You do know we have an extra pair of boots in the tack room if Blake wants them?" She giggles the whole time she speaks.

"No. I think he's fine."

She laughs so hard. "You are so mean, Amity Jean!"

"Not mean, but hell, everyone's gotta learn somehow. He probably thinks it's a walk in the park because he wore sneakers in Costa Rica because we were hiking when we were on the horses. He shouldn't even be here anyways."

"Well, he is. And he's here because of you. So, try not to throw him in a stampede today."

"No promises." I cluck my tongue at Nevada to get moving.

Dirks calls my name. "Amity, I have you and Blake with guests Mr. Hutchinson, his wife, Jessica, and the Witt family. So, a total of five guests are your and Blake's responsibility today on top of the cattle. Y'all be my drags."

"What? I should be swing."

Gritting his teeth, he says, "I need you to be drag today. No big deal. I have Willow and Nash as my swings with their guests. Tilly and Jose are my points with Carlos and Bekah as my flanks."

"Howdy partner." Rolling my eyes at the return of Blake, who just rode up next to me. "Here is your hat, darlin' and your saddle pack."

"Thanks." Taking it from him, I turn around to quickly fasten it through the buckle. "Did you hear Dirks? You're in the back with me and five guests."

"Let's ride out to the sunrise together," he jokes.

Without lookin' over to him, I make kiss sounds to Nevada, and he takes off in a canter toward the pasture. "Such a good boy" I say, rubbing his neck down. Slowing down while we all get in position to start moving cattle, Blake catches up to me along with our five people.

"You can't just be taken off today, Amity."

"I have more experience. You should know when to keep up and not get lost or left behind." Turning to the five people, I direct the Hutchisons to my left, the Witts to my right, and Blake, I send to the other side of the Witts. "These are your spots. You do not want to get too close or be too far back. Always be prepared and on the lookout. We do have walkie-talkies," I hold mine up, "so if anything, concerning happens in front of us, we will definitely be told back here to prepare. If for some reason I take off, you do not need to follow unless I tell you to follow. Sometimes herds scatter and cows go into the brush, especially the young ones. I need you all to stay put and control the back. Everyone good? Ready?" They nod with a couple of yee-haws. I can see the fear but excitement on their faces. "I promise y'all this will be an experience of a lifetime, just always be on notice. All right y'all, let's go." Blake throws his hands up at me as if I was just sending him to the other side of the world.

A grin peeks through my poker face.

BLAKE

Three hours in with no sign of other life beyond the rolling hills of grass and trees. Just cows and cow asses with tails swinging, staring back at me. Strangers to my left, no one to my right. My girl is far on the other side avoiding me.

My feet are killing me. I knew I should've taken Nash's offer to wear his old worn boots. But I've had these sitting in the box waiting to impress Amity at some point. Probably would've been better to take her out on a date in these and not spend my day bumping and grinding against a horse and pushing my feet against stirrups. The morning has been fairly uneventful. Only one calf attempted to wander off, but badass Tilly was on him. I am just over here having random conversations with myself. Or maybe with a few cows. They seem to moo at me every so often, either in encouragement or telling me to shut the hell up.. *Oh good it looks like we're stopping for a bit. Please don't let it be like a YellowStone, and they all just scatter, and we have to round them up before we get going again!* I think in my head.

Riding over to Amity, I hear through her walkie-talkie we have an hour to rest. Let the cows graze as the guests stretch their legs and take pictures. I come up to the side of her horse and slowly dismount mine onto my aching feet. Tying him up next to hers. "That was something," I say to grab her attention. She side-eyes me then looks away. Impulse has me grabbing her arm and yanking her behind the overgrown tree out of sight. I lean in, blocking her with my arms and body and looking down at her stunning face. "About last night…"

"What about it?"

"Can we talk about it?"

She shrugs her shoulders. "Sure. We had dinner. I let you fuck me into oblivion. I slapped you, had a temporary break of insanity, cried, and fell asleep."

Nodding, I shift my feet. "That pretty much sums up the evening. Do you remember what I said to you?"

She hesitates then meets my eyes. "No."

"How do you forget when someone tells you, *I love you.*"

"I forget when I don't believe. Blake, my trust in you is shattered. My love for you is splintered. I don't know how I can forgive you. I still don't even know what the hell happened to even understand how we got here."

My brain seems to think now's better than any to let her in on the issue. Though my heart is telling me not to. Unfortunately, my mouth opens before I can debate my next move. "I have a file on you, Amity." I pause, letting that nibble of information set in.

"You what? How do you have a file on me, and why would you?"

"Holdings protocol. Nash had to do the same thing with Willa. Though she is like an open book where you are a book with torn out chapters." If looks could kill, I would already be six feet in the ground. "I freaked the fuck out, Amity. How could you not tell me about him? How could you not tell me you were married before?" She is turning red and flustered, her lips going in a straight line while I glance at her fingers flexing into fists.

"You invaded my privacy without even asking. How could you? And then you find out and leave instead of trusting me enough to just fucking ask? Jesus' pineapples, Blake, what the hell is wrong with you?"

"I know. And I know I keep saying I know because I fucking know! And I can't apologize enough. But I wanted it to be a surprise. We don't pull information until we're ready to make that type of commitment. I planned on proposing to you before I left. But Nash wanted answers about the file from you. And I was selfish enough to not see you. To not have our last night ruined with all of this bullshit instead of making it a memorable evening by asking you to marry me." Piercing blue eyes are wide-open with her mouth gawking at me.

"Oh, I can't even with you right now…so… Let me get this straight… You wanted me to marry you?" I nod in response. "But you had information dug up on me that revealed some incident from my past?" I'm nodding again. "And you thought it was best to leave the country? Not call or text or have any communication with me whatsoever for several weeks?"

"Well when you put it like that it sounds a lot worse than in my head."

"It sounds a lot worse, Blake, because it's that ridiculous. You were my best friend. I trusted you with *my* everything! You know damn well I don't do knights in shining armor, grand gestures, or believe in fairytales. But you have me creating one with you." A tear slips down her cheek, I go to wipe it with my thumb. "Don't," she growls out. "You don't get to touch me. You don't get to care for me or love me. You don't get to say what I do or who I do anymore. You were my person until you weren't. You may only dream about me because that's the closest you are ever going to get again."

Pushing me away from her, Amity stomps off, and I don't have the grit in me to stop her this time.

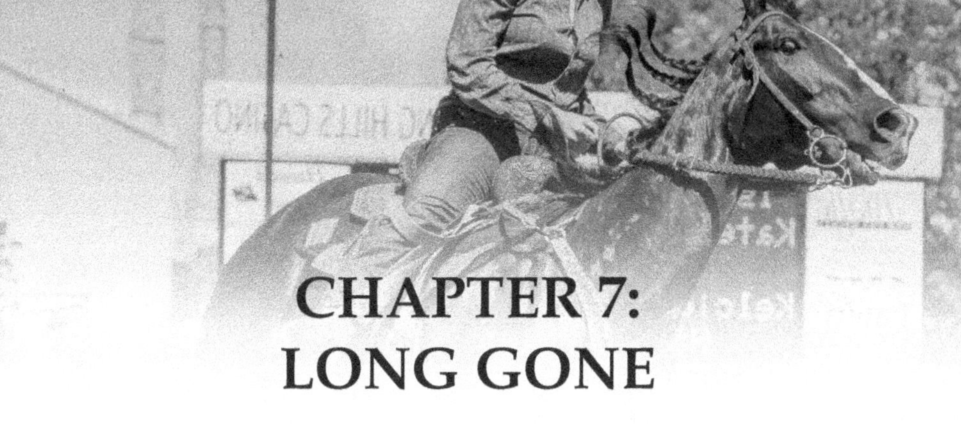

CHAPTER 7:
LONG GONE

Four hours later we made it to the new pasture, where the cattle will be spending the next week, until we do it all over again next Sunday. Then we keep them at the ranch for three weeks for vaccinations and checkups. Now, I have sixty less heads to worry about on the way back to the ranch. Though, we are taking a break for lunch and rest.

"Tilly, what was so damn funny?" Willa asks.

"What are you talking about?" She looks back at me, causing me to laugh.

"Damn you two. Y'all went on your own channel to chat. I figured, every time a loud laugh would blow through the wind toward me."

"Tilly! Stay off the radio!" Dirks yells over to her.

"OOOOO, someone is getting a spanking from her boyfriend later."

"O my hades, gross, Amity. They are not together." All I can do is laugh, while Tilly slams her mouth shut and glares at me.

"So, what or who were you two gossiping about?"

"Mostly Nash, because I thought he was goin' to fall off at one point tryin' to keep up with you. But then we talked about Blake," I say.

"Please enlighten me."

"The usual, but usual with admiration for both their asses in jeans. Blake looks like a damn model that just stepped out a Stetson magazine. How can that piece of meat not be pinned over? Look, even the old ladies are checking both of them out." The girls giggle at the sight.

"Nash can't be wearing his Wranglers in public anymore. Literally a woman at Albertsons ran smack into the snack display, toppling the whole thing over, because she couldn't stop drooling and staring at him. It was embarrassing." We laugh so loud, drawing all the attention to us. "The Holdings are a fine-looking bunch. Even the older one, Clint. I'm surprised he hasn't been snatched up yet."

"He loves his work too much. Nash is the same way, but we have set limits when it comes to him working all the time. But Clint, he has no care about taking a night off, to go on a vacation or relax. But I have heard rumors of him going to secret sex clubs and is a fierce predator in the bedroom."

Tilly and I look at her stunned. I think through the ones I've been to and don't recall him. Then decide to not embed that in my head for the time being. "Hmmmm, good way not to get hurt either. Devote your life to something that will not fail you," I say.

"What's the fun in that though?" Tilly asks.

I shrug my shoulders. "I can have enough fun on my own."

"That is one thing we know for sure, honey," Willa states while laying out our blanket to sit on. Reeling in how great sitting down on solid ground feels for a few minutes, I look over at Willa and Tilly laughing over something, and behind them, the guests fade into the cattle that fade into the trees. Off to our left the young and old cowboys mingle and talk about life.

"Hey, Wil. How did you feel when Nash pulled a file on you?" She gawks at me, like I have two heads.

"Amity, are you trying to tell me something? Because though I tell you everything, I don't think that has ever been brought up, due to Nash asking me to keep quiet on it."

Taking a deep breath, I let it out. "You were right, what Nash was keeping from you was about me. Blake was going to propose, until they dug up my past." Both her and Tilly turn ghost white.

"Wait, you telling me he was going to propose until he found out about him? Or was he going to propose until he read your file and about him?" Tilly asks in her own way.

"I think both," I nod, pinching my eyebrows together. "He said he freaked out and didn't want to ruin our last night together, panicked and left. But yes, I think he was goin' to propose until he found out about him."

"That son of a bitch. I'm going to taser Nash and kill Blake."

"Calm down, girl," I murmur, patting Willa on the shoulder. "It is what it is at this point. Blake found out, freaked the fuck out, and left. Just like any rational man would do, right?"

"I wouldn't say rational," Willa chimes in.

"Or reasonable," both girls say.

Willa chunks an orange at Nash and nails him right in the head, causing their circle to turn around and gawk at us. Willa motions her finger to come over with the look of "alone" written on her face.

"Pineapples, Willa, don't confront him here," I admonish, gritting my teeth. Only for her to roll her eyes at me.

As soon as he steps into our circle, she goes in for the kill. "I swear by Persephone and Demeter, Nash, I will taser you in the ball sac if you lie to me." The look of worry trickles down his face. "You pulled a file on Amity and didn't tell me or have Blake ask her. There are secrets

Amity has tried to hide from, and then Blake finds out on a whim with no one questioning anything? Just disappearing to South America! And you don't say a damn word to me about it? I have half a mind to drag you to the middle of the pasture and cause a stampede over you right now!"

"Jesus, Willa." Putting his hands up, he calls defeat. "Look, yes, that all happened. You know damn well I couldn't tell you at the time, and honestly, I didn't think it would be drawn out for so long. Hindsight, bad call on my part."

"You think?" we all say in unison.

"I'm sorry, Amity, really, I am. I have my own questions and concerns, but I know Blake loves you. I demanded he not propose to you before we had answers. Not because we do not love you, but I have to protect the company and family name. Need to know of enemies. The last thing I wanted was this to feel like a personal attack on you. Unfortunately, I see now that is exactly what has happened. I truly am sorry."

I step in to give him a hug. "Thank you for owning your shit, Nash. And I am happy to discuss the things you read in the file."

"You don't owe me that, Amity. I do hope you talk to Blake though. Even with the findings, he still wanted to propose. His feelings or wanting to be with you never faltered once. Please know that."

"Thanks. Um, I'll think about it." We hear Dirks' loud whistle, knowing the time has come to head back to the ranch. We split off to our horses, and feeling overwhelmed with new emotion and information, I strive to get back as quickly as I can.

Once Nevada is released into the pasture, I holler at the girls that I'm leaving.

"Amity, wait. Can we go talk somewhere?" Blake asks over filling the water troughs.

"Can't. I have a date with Jack tonight."

"Jack who?"

"You know damn well what Jack I'm talkin' about!" I turn to leave, getting in my truck before he thinks about following me. Blake's face comes into my rearview as I drive off. *Not tonight, Cowboy.* I don't even care to stop by my apartment to change tonight. I got an extra flannel top in my truck that I pull over my pink tank top and leave open. Throwing my hair in a low twisted tail so out of my face, I put my poker face on as I walk into Dan's Bar ready to drink my sorrows away.

Jack keeps me company for about six rounds until someone offers me Jose, and now, I have a new best friend. "Ha! There is a reason why tequila and I don't get along," I say to the guy who offered the shot. "I guess this bar is going to find out why tonight!" Throwing back another shot. His hand slides up my inner thigh as if he's thinking that's the direction I'm heading in. "I'm going to need you to remove your hand from my body."

"Come on girl, we're just all trying to have a good time." Grabbing his hand then wrenching his wrist backwards until I see the water swell up in his eyes, I snap, "I warned you once. Don't make me full on kick your ass next time." Letting go of his hand, he pulls it back to hold it against his body in pain. I turn back around to my favorite bartender Dan himself. With a smile only a devil can deem good.

"Don't give me no problems tonight, Amity!"

"Who? Little ol' me? The night is just getting started, Dan."

"That's what I'm afraid of," he mutters and walks off, continuing to wipe down the bar and serve a customer down ways.

At some point, my hair has made it into a messy bun on top of my head, and I am pouring sweat from all the dancing. I know I've been on stage and sung at least a dozen songs tonight, but all seems like a blur. But damn does this cold bathroom tile feel amazing against my skin.

BLAKE

It's one in the morning when I shoot out of bed due to heavy banging on my front door. Peeking through the hole, I notice it's Willa, Tilly, Lana, and Nash. "What is this some kind of intervention? It's damn one o'clock in the morning," I groan, opening the door.

"Not so much an intervention for you. Possibly Amity. We need to go, *like* now," Tilly speaks up. A coldness rushes over me while panic takes over.

"Is she alright? What the Hell's going on?"

Willa steps in. "I will explain everything in the car. Right now, we need to get in the car and get to her ASAP." I quickly shove on a pair of jeans, a hoodie, and grab my boots from earlier, and fly out the door behind them.

Once in the car I look at the four of them. "Start explaining now!"

"So, Amity went to Dan's Bar tonight and had a really good time with Jack and Jose."

"You mean the fucking drinks, not men, right?" Tilly giggles, nodding her head yes, like I asked a dumb question. I'm thinking we are talking about Amity; this conversation could go either way.

"Y'all told me she's not supposed to drink that shit, and she's good about not drinking that shit."

"Yeah. But she's pretty unpredictable these days. Dan stated she was offered a shot of tequila, and it went downhill from there. Um, then she hurt the guy's hand that offered her the shot because I guess he touched her." Fury ramps up the heat in my body. Because how dare anybody touch my girl. "Then she got in a fight with another dude and broke his nose. She did a lot of dancing with everyone. She apparently has been partying like a rockstar on stage singing tonight. Broke a barstool on the bar itself to fight like a pirate against a group of guys that were trying to, as she put it to Dan, "manhandle" her. Then Dan said they were just trying to capture her, to tie her up to not cause any more mischief for the night until we got there."

"So, what you're telling me is tequila makes her crazy and angry, and she's had plenty of it tonight."

"Yep, that about sums it up." I am first going to murder them for trying to touch her, and then I might kill her myself for acting like such a damn fool. Nash is driving like a madman and gets us there in under fifteen minutes from my apartment. All the while, I don't know if I need to pump myself up for what I'm about to walk into or calm my shit before I piss her off even more.

Once we walk into the bar, Dan waves us over. "She is currently in the bathroom. Cassidy went in there to check on her and found her vomiting. Which, hell, probably is the best for her at this point," he says. I had walked in ready to ravage several men that touched my girl tonight, but once I got a glimpse of the scene of a broken barstool, the dude nursing his nose, and another with a swollen black eye, all I can do is laugh and think *my girl did that*. She is a fucking force to be reckoned with sober or drunk.

So I subtly walk over to them, shake their hands, and say, "I'm not even going to kick your ass because you've partly already had one handed to you tonight, but on the other hand, don't fucking put your hands on her again because if she didn't teach you a lesson, I sure and hell will the next go round." They nod and turn to leave.

Sliding my black card over to Dan, I tell him, "Please put her tab and whatever damage she's done tonight on this."

"Thanks man."

Turning back to the gang, I laugh. "She is the craziest ass woman I have ever met." I get a glare from Willa, Lana, and Tilly. "Y'all know damn well what crazy I'm talking about. Who else do you know will beat up a bunch of bar guys and break a barstool because she's drinking tequila. And the sad thing is I don't think she needed the tequila to even accomplish that!" They all try to suppress their laughs, because I think we could all be pissed to tears at this point over the truth.

I then follow the ladies into the women's bathroom to see two legs sticking out of the stall with the door open. I try hard not to laugh my ass off because she is sitting up against the toilet, hair on top of her head. A complete disoriented mess, but just as beautiful and adorable. The girls speak softly to her, so she knows who is with her, and then I help lift her off the ground.

"Oh my favorite people," Amity squeals. "Except for you," she grumbles, looking directly at me, then pointing her middle finger at me. "You're not my favorite people anymore."

"Come on, Amity. We will deal with you and me later. Let's just get you home," I say as calmly as I can.

"No. I'm not goin' anywhere with you. I just spent the last hour throwin' your name across the bathroom floor. This is your fault."

Being the gentleman I am, I allow what she says to slide. "I take full responsibility. Only if you admit you were wrong to hang out with Jose Cuervo tonight."

She gives me a wink. "At least he wasn't scared to commit and promised to give me exactly what I expected."

"Ah fuck!" I run my hand through my hair and back down my face in anguish.

Tilly whispers, "We have her, go." Knowing this is not the time or place to have it out with her, I walk out the door and over to the bar to grab my card and sign the bill.

"Twenty-six hundred dollars?!? Who the hell racks up a tab like that at the bar?" I shout.

"That would be Amity. I'm only charging you three hundred for the bar stool and gap she left in my bar. She did buy several rounds of shots for the dance floor and band." Shaking my head in disbelief, I squiggle my name on the bill. This woman is going to be the damn death of me. Turning back around to say something to Nash, I see Amity sitting in the middle of the empty dance floor, crisscrossed with her face in palms. Lana tries to get her to drink some water while Willa tries to calm her down.

I walk over and bend down to be face-to-face, lifting her chin up to face me. She looks up at me with those cold ice dagger eyes, and it's like I fall in love all over again.

"Hey, princess, why don't we get you home."

Through tears and heavy sobbing, she cries, "I am so sorry, Blake. For everything and anything I did to make you feel like it was best to walk away. I hate my past, but I can't change it."

"Let's talk about this tomorrow after you have some sleep, I'm not going anywhere." She nods as I pull her up to stand with me. "Maybe you'll remember this in the morning, maybe not, but I love you, Amity Jean, regardless of your past or the present by being victimized by a bar's bathroom floor." The gang laughs at my attempt for a subtle joke.

Looking over at Willa, I ask, "Please tell me we have towels or blankets to wrap around her before we get in the car?"

The four of them laugh again, because my Germaphobia of public restrooms is a joke to them. But I'm cringing on the inside, making a mental note to put Amity in the shower as soon as we reach my apartment.

Nash is slightly calmer driving back to my apartment now that we have Amity with us and safe. She has fallen asleep on my shoulder, but not before she whispered how much she has missed me since I left. How much she loves me. But also, how much she hates me right now. I completely understand as I pulled her into my world and had her give me her heart that I shattered. *How do we get back from here?*

The crew helps me get her up to the apartment, and the girls decide to go help her in the shower while Nash and I have a talk. "Anything happen today that might've triggered her 'don't give a damn' attitude?" he asks.

Deep breath in, I blow it out slowly, puffing out my cheeks. "I told her about the file, then that I was going to ask her to marry me, but then chickened out and left because I'm a selfish prick." Nash slips his drink slowly with his gaze down.

"Just say it, bro. I am a fuck up and ruined whatever business we have going on in Brazil on top of ruining whatever chance I had with Amity."

"No. Not what I was going to say. Business is fine and will be fine until you get back down there. Which needs to be this week. I hadn't had a chance to talk to you after the cattle drive, but I knew you said something to Amity because I was ambushed by three of the Golden Girls." I see a glint of fear still lingering in his eyes. "As far as Amity goes, at least you got the hardest part out of the way which was confessing. Now prove to her that she is enough for you and herself. We did some more digging. The guy behind all this lives down in El Paso, living on family money and laundered money. He apparently is still well known, with lots of connections and has quite a few assets. Something to consider if she really needs the next step to move forward. Or you can do absolutely nothing with this bit of information. Just thought you should have it."

"Thanks, brother!" We clink our glasses together, and Nash toasts to love. I'm just hoping I still have my girl after all of this.

The ladies come out to the kitchen, letting me know Amity is all cleaned up, hair dried, and tucked in bed. I thank them, then walk them to the door. Once we say goodbyes and I shut the door, I pad back to my bathroom for a quick shower. Once out, I head to the bedroom where the nightstand's lamp is still on, putting the perfect cast of light over Amity's features. Standing over her, I'm unsure what to say or do next. Something that used to be so easy when it came to us being together, now has all my caution bells ringing because I'm unsure of how she will react if I get too close or stay too far away.

As she was reading my mind, I see her eyes flutter open, then she pulls the covers back. "Come to bed, babe. Tomorrow's another day." I crawl into bed and hold her, having the best sleep, I've had since I left.

CHAPTER 8:
GETTING LOST

All I wanted last night was a sense of belonging and peace with whom captured my heart. The only way I knew how was to lie next to Blake, breathing in his juniper scent with our skin caressing each other. I need all this before I walk away from him for good, but not before I share my story. He deserves that from me, and then he can hop on the next plane to Brazil. Blake has five more months out there. Five months I don't want to hold either of us accountable to promises that may not even exist anymore. Maybe after his time away, he will show up at my door, still wanting me. Still needing me like air. Still loving me as if his heart is breaking in two without me. *A girl can always dream, right?* We both need this time to figure out what future promises we want for ourselves and for each other. If any at all.

I roll over, placing my head in the nook of his arm and chest. His breathing is steady, but with instinct, his arm wraps around my body, holding me close to his. My eyes trail down his rippled stomach down to the bulge in briefs. I slowly trace my finger down the path my eyes made, through his manscaped happy trail, teasing the band on his briefs. His breath hitches slightly, but his eyes stay closed. Slowly, I slip my hand into his briefs, gently touching and gliding my hand up his shaft. "Damn, I love you," Blake whispers out, almost making me freeze in motion as I was not expecting those words to spill from his lips. But dammit, pineapples. The butterflies take flight from the pit of my stomach, and I inch my body down his, kissing his bare chest as I go. Running my palms all over his body, remembering every freckle, ripple, and scar like this will be my last time with him.

BLAKE

My girl knows how to wake me up in the morning. Nothing else beats her body next to mine, and then her mouth engulfing my cock while she squeezes my sac. She takes me in deep as her tongue circles around and teases the tip before pulling back. Only to do it over and over again. O, god, she…"shit," I groan out in pleasure. She uses her teeth to bare down on me before grinding them in a back and forth motion to cause just enough pressure, and it feels so fucking good.

"Amity, baby, let me have you. Let me come inside you." My mouth says one thing, but my hand is wrapped in her hair guiding her back and forth on my cock. Not that she needs it, but her mouth feels incredible. All my dick wants to do is enjoy all the pleasure for himself and explode down her throat. She pulls back and makes a "pop" noise, pulling her mouth off my pied piper. *Yes, I love that nickname.* Our eyes connect, and I move faster than a cheetah going in for the kill, flipping her on her back. Not even giving her a millisecond to think, I push into her core.

Amity yells, "holy shit!" as she instinctively wraps her legs around my waist and digs her claws into my ass cheeks to hold on. Bucking against me, meeting my moan for moan. I am completely, devastatingly obsessed with this woman underneath me. Letting her go will never be an option. Not now, not ever. Her body tensing pulls me back to her ice dagger eyes and dark hair splayed out over the bed. Amity's beauty is captivating. Her fearlessness is riveting. Her heart, body, and soul…mine! I slow my pace down, drawing out a moan of ecstasy. Pushing her to beg me, "please. Blake." Panting, "hard, fast." I know I am on the precipice myself, so I give my girl what she wants. Pulling her legs up, with her feet resting on my shoulders, I thrust hard into her. It only takes a few movements, before she clenches over me, squeezing my shaft, with me spilling inside her, making her moan even louder.

"You are mine, Amity. Only mine," I whisper. Claiming all of her, while I continue to slowly grind, allowing my release to subside in her.

Letting her legs go, falling onto the bed on either side of my body, I hover over her. Brushing my hand through her hair, kissing her breasts, up to her neck, cheek then lips. "Know this one thing, Amity. I love you. Only you and me. Got it?" She nods her head yes, and her eyes swell with tears, making her eyes look like pristine glaciers floating across water. Lying next to her, I pull her against my body to hold her tightly. Reeling in that only I ever see this rare emotional side of her. She is such a hard-ass all day long with everyone, but I cherish these tears, even if she is hurting. "Baby, all will be okay. We are going to figure this out. I promise you."

Amity rolls over to face me. "I don't think any of this will be okay. Not after how I tell you how damaged I am." Just like that, in Amity fashion, she begins to spill the tea on the history I could give two shitting cows about, but I sense the importance to her to tell me.

CHAPTER 9:
BACK WHEN

"My ex-husband's name is Gage. Gage Hendrix. We actually grew up together, though he lived a few streets over with high society. Away from the trailer park road I was living on with my asshole sperm donor, Herb. Gage was always charming and looked out for me, as I didn't live in the best of neighborhoods. He was just always around. I won't lie either. He was cute, but he grew up to be a stunning man that exuded power and demanded attention. It was appealing, even more so, because I knew him better than most. For so many years we were each other's confidants. We were best friends and kept in touch when my mom and I finally left and moved here with Stan. Gage would come out here in the summer to hang for a few days at a time. Always made a point to be at most of my rodeos, and yah, he was my first kiss, my first…" I notice Blake's jaw clenching and decide to not dive into details. "Yah, he was a lot of firsts for me. So, he didn't just come out of the blue one day asking for my hand. Though it did kinda feel like it, lookin' back."

I sit up and Blake follows my lead, still sitting in front of me, with his hands on my thighs. I grab a pillow to place in front of my naked body due to the uneasiness this conversation is bringing.

"He did show up one day, explaining to me who his dad really was. Mr. Birsha himself. Everyone knew the name, but no one really knew who the man was behind the name. He always had his lackeys to hide behind, and I've always known Gage's dad as a nice man, good father, a church-going man. Hell, he had my vote for any category against Herb. Anyways, Mr. Birsha was a huge loan shark, and apparently the man I lived with owed him a substantial amount of money. Like we are talking hundreds of thousands he had racked up overtime plus interest. Gage told me his father had plans to murder mine. Back then, I had a little more heart and thought it would be awful for my own "dad" to be murdered because he was a battered old rodeo cowboy who spent his days doing odd jobs when he wasn't too drunk. Stan and my mom always enjoyed Gage's company and thought well of him. Enough for even around the same time, Stan confided in Gage about how bad the ranch was struggling to the point he wasn't sure he would be able to hold on to it. I guess his master plan came together so much easier than even he expected."

I take a deep breath and fist the pillow a little tighter.

"He laid the proposal out on the table to my parents and me. Confessing even to them who his dad was. He confessed his feelings for me, but most of all, my dad would be safe, and he would be able to help my parents keep the ranch, because we would be family. And no one hurts his family. I was young and stupid. Thought I loved him. Believed he loved me. I've lived the life of a poor child, a blue-collar teenager, fighting and earning her way in the world. I earned my scholarship that put me through college, and for that, I am so thankful for. But I had a chance to be a wife to a rich man. To a powerful man and not have to want for nothing."

Blake rolls his eyes with annoyance. "You don't get to do that," I spout at him. "You have never wanted anything you knew you could never have. Never known the feeling of hunger or wondering if your dad is going to be dead the next morning when you woke up, because he drank himself into a stupor. So yah, I was being selfish for once, and it was going to benefit the people I loved. The girls thought I was crazy but stood by my side anyway. It was a huge lavish wedding in May after graduation. His dad covered all expenses and gave me a brand-new Audi for a wedding gift. Along with covering costs on a brand-new apartment for college for the next four years so I didn't have to live in the dorms. He had pull, and no one questioned him. Not even me, especially knowing who he was. But he called me the daughter he never had and treated me like a princess. For a few months, that is exactly what I felt like. Gage was attentive as I lived with him before going off to college. He sent Herb to rehab, paid off Stan's ranch loan, never asking for a thing. I played the dutiful wife for the summer. Waited on Gage hand and foot. Always had dinner ready, though half the time I ate alone. Whatever he wanted I let him take. He saved my family, treated me well, and I was heading off to college. Wasn't until I went off to college that everything shifted. He rarely wanted to travel to Oklahoma to see me, so I made a point to come home when I didn't have a rodeo to attend. It was maybe the third weekend I came home in September that I realized he was taking over his father's loan business. Stepping out to be the next Mr. Birsha. I told him I did not think it was a great idea, because I worried about him. We ended up in a huge fight with a gun pointed to my head."

Blake shoots out of bed when his fists clenched. Turning to me, he grits out, "Keep going," as he begins to pace across the room, naked.

"Um, well right after, he turned me around, slammed me into the wall, and took me from behind as he held the barrel to my back. Telling me he owned me.

Pulling my hair so hard, I thought I was going to have bald spots on my scalp. He cussed me the whole time, saying I was nothing but a bitch, whoring it up at school. A horrible worthless wife by not being home with him."

Blake swings at the standing mirror, splintering the glass. I lurch out of bed with a scream. He comes running over to me. "I'm so sorry baby, I didn't mean to scare you. I am just infuriated that this happened, and I know this story is going to get worse. I just want to protect you from all of it." He holds onto me like a starved attention child finding shelter in the arms of a loved one.

After several minutes, he releases me. I go throw on his t-shirt while he throws on a pair of athletic shorts, and we make our way to the kitchen. I begin again, while wetting a rag for his hand to clean the blood. "It did get worse. He would show up randomly at school, pulling me out of class just to have sex. Putting his claim on me around campus. Then he would turn around and buy me a new bag or jewelry to make up for being a bastard. Only to do it all over again. Gage was just so angry all the time because I wasn't home. He was threatening Stan to return all the money he had gifted them for the ranch because his daughter was a jezebel. It was not until later I found out he had his goonies beat Stan up and scare my mom every chance they had. With the previous loan paid off, he re-financed the ranch to pay Gage off and that seemed to infuriate him even more."

"Gage demanded my parents pay interest and collected half their income weekly for the next several months. Mom never told me until they were about to lose the property again because Gage had put a financial strain on them. He also stopped paying for Herb's rehab, leaving him to be kicked to the streets. When I came home for winter break for three weeks, that was when it escalated further. I found out he had several girls on the side along with confirming he was geek-ing out on cocaine most days. For some reason, one night, after several glasses of wine, I told him he needed to choose. Either me or his lifestyle. Gage brought a knife to my throat and threatened to skin me alive."

I raise my shirt up enough to show the tally marks down my side. I've had treatments to make them less visible, so unless you know they are there, you don't know to look. To anyone looking at my tan skin, they might even pass off as stretch marks with a quick glance.

Blake comes in closer, bending down and leaning in. His finger presses into the first one as he begins to trace each one, counting under his breath. My body tenses under each touch. "Twelve." He stands back up, nose to nose now. "Twelve marks, Amity. For the love of God, why were you marked?"

"Each one is for when he felt I needed to be put in place. And it's actually thirteen." Guiding his hand, I move him a little lower down my waist to my tan line. "This was the last one he was able to complete. His father just happened to stop by the house one February weekend I was home. Except Gage had me tied to the bed, naked and gagged. He was carving this last one in, causing me to bleed all over the bed. He was shouting, slapping me in the face. Never heard his father enter our bedroom. Didn't even know he was there myself until I saw him charge Gage, shoving him off the opposite side of the bed. Gage was too strong along with rage and the coke, he was able to remove himself from his father's headlock. Pulling the gun out from under his pillow, Gage shot and killed his own father. The guards rushed into the room at this point, taking in the whole scene. They quickly brought him to his knees and handcuffed until he calmed down and realized what he did."

The scene flashes through my mind the moment the Gage I had known came to tuition of the damage he caused once sober. He cried and cried. I broke when he cried in my lap begging me for forgiveness, telling me how much he loved me. To me the damage was done.

I feel hands on my arms. "Amity, hey. If this is too much…" I stop him.

"No, I'm fine, just havin' a flashback…but yah, um. Gage finally sobered and realized he murdered his father and tortured me all in one night. For me, my heart turned stone and could feel absolutely nothin'. There was nothin' Gage could say or do to change my mind. I left the next day for home battered and bruised. Found out all the shit I said earlier, and a switch flipped inside me. Torturing me is one thing, but he fucked with my family, Blake. Sperm donor showed up weeks later dead in a ditch, my parents were about to lose everything on top of fearing for their lives. A few days after and ignoring Gage's calls, I went back to school to sell my apartment along with everything inside. Picked up a waitressing job to help survive through the semester and sendin' back home what I could. I was killin' myself to get my education, working every shift I could to make ends meet. Tryin' to keep my grades up, rodeo practice, and competitions. I had Lana there, but no one else. She tried to help, but it all just became too much for the both of us. I started taking uppers just to stay awake through the day. By the time the semester ended, I lost all ambition for life.

"The school gave me some grace but told me I would be put on academic suspension in the fall if I didn't come back with my shit together. Lana came home for the summer, but my apartment still hadn't sold, so I decided to stay there until it did. Which led to partying all night, experimenting sexually just to try to feel something. Ask the girls, they will tell you I was in a dark place. Gage had finally stopped calling, but I also had no idea where he was, leaving me in fear." I walk over to the opposite counter to start the coffee.

"End of August that year, I was served divorce papers with a note from him. Stating that he would always love me, but he needed to cut ties until he got his shit together and was leaving town. He gave me the deed to the house and my apartment to do as I wished. Paid my parents back all the money they paid him on and in the letter apologized about Herb. That he would live with all the guilt and pain he caused me. All with the undertone of him returning. Even had the nerve stating he would pay for any therapy I may need, just reach out to his lawyer," I say with a huff, still pissed, he felt he had the audacity to say such a thing to me.

Blake is sitting across from me sipping his coffee slowly, drinking all this information in. "I signed the papers the same day, never had to go to court to finalize. I just received a letter a week later with a bouquet of yellow roses that was all signed and complete. I sold our house and my car. Invested half, buried Herb's ashes in his family's cemetery, bought my truck, quit my job, and lived off the rest like a frugal person." Shrugging my shoulders, I know to some it was a big deal, but not to me. "Not like I knew any difference anyhow. Once I finally graduated, I sold the apartment, moved back to town, and bought the one I am in now. Donated a chunk to a local women's shelter. Then I bought my horse, Nevada. Honestly, I don't have to work. Between my savings and investments, I am worth a few million. My parents are too proud, so they won't take a dime from me. I splurge on one trip every other year but love my girl weekends away. The girls don't even know how much money I have. They have never asked what I did with all the money. Honestly, they probably think I created a bonfire out of dollar bills. I enjoy my job at the college though and helping at the ranch. It fulfills a part of me that I was missing through the early years of all hell and coping." I pause and find Blake gaping at me.

"Surely you knew the money part, being that you have dug up information on me that I paid good money to hide."

"No, I didn't. Come to think back, Nash never gave me your financial file. Probably thought I couldn't handle that on top of the news of you being married."

"Well, now you know my story and baggage. So…yah." Walking away, I place my cup in the sink, avoiding looking directly at Blake. I soon feel him behind me, wrapping his arms around my chest, pulling me into him. He kisses the top of my head.

"Amity, you have been unflinchingly honest with me. Thank you." He pauses his thoughts and kisses the top of my head again. "I won't apologize for all that shit you went through because I have no control over any of that time, but I am certain your path brought you to me. I wish I could wipe away your scars and pain. I promise though to kiss away your tears and fight for your love every single day." Turning me to face him, then picking me up to sit on the counter, he maneuvers himself between my legs. "You, my love, are a badass. Yes, you are mouthy and feisty, but those are parts I appreciate about you. You hold your own in bar fights and a force to be reckoned with daily. I am truly the luckiest guy ever to be in your circle and to be loved by you. Call me crazy, but…" Before I can blink, Blake is down on one knee in front of me, practically naked in the middle of his kitchen.

BLAKE

"Amity Jean Mercer, will you marry me? Wake me up every morning with a blow job and let me pound you every night into oblivion. Let me love and cherish you in all the ways you deserve for infinity. You are mine in every way possible already, now be my wife in front of God, our friends and family, and to the whole world."

She is giggling with tears streaming down her face, leaving me waiting. Time is slowly ticking by, before she hops off the counter and tackles me to the floor. Straddling me, she shouts, "Yes, a thousand percent yes!" Placing my hands on her face, I pull her down to me and seize her mouth with mine. Our tongues dancing together in perfection. Pulling away from her, I lift her shirt over her head then roll us over, so she is bare on the cold tile floor. Looking into her eyes, my heart skips several beats at the beauty she possesses.

"Damn, I love you," I whisper before kissing down her neck, down her chest, sucking her nipples into my mouth as my hand slides down her stomach to tease her heat. She is already soaked for me, ready for me. I bit down on her right nipple, causing her to let out a loud moan. "Pain and pleasure, baby, just the way you want me. First, I need to taste you." My mouth is already salivating before I reach her pussy. Glistening pink folds are just for me. Bending her legs up over my arms, I drag her by her ass across the floor, closer to my mouth. As soon as my tongue slides between her folds, I become a starving man for her and her alone. Licking and lapping up her sweetness, pushing her over the edge with my fingers circling her clit.

"Damn pineapples, Blake. O… My… Don't St..." My mouth hungrily nibbles on her between the deep tongue lashings. Amity's body trembles when my tongue goes rigid and flicks against her clit over and over again. Right when I know she cusps the edge of release, I stop. My eyes meet her ice daggers that look to stab me for leaving her on the edge.

"Don't worry, baby, I have you." She trails her fingers down my chest, but I grab her hands, crawling on top of her. Pinning each wrist down, I tease her entrance with my cock. She huffs impatiently at me, but I know I have her exactly where I want her. *Desperate*. I bury myself inside of her to the hilt, letting out a low deep groan, knowing I won't last much longer.

"Amity," I grunt out while she meets me thrust for thrust. She claws my back shouting my name, and it's the most serene sound. "Amity, I need you to come now." Her back arches, and I feel her pulse around my shaft as my own release begins to fill her. "I. fucking. love. you," I pant out between breaths, slowing down my pace and drawing out my time inside.

"I love you more," she says, pulling my face down toward hers to kiss me.

CHAPTER 10:
FAST-ER

"Holy fuck balls! I'm engaged to playboy, Blake Holdings!" I whisper under my breath, staring at my bottle of water, letting the waves of emotion crash over me. Blake must hear me because he lets out his sinister laugh before picking me up at the waist and swinging me around.

"You are. But it's me with all the bragging rights," he cackles, followed by his Cheshire grin.

Shaking my head and laughing, I look back up to him, "So do we call our friends and family now?"

"No, first I need to go pick up your ring, then we will stop by my parents for lunch and friends for dinner?"

"That works for me. That means I need to ignore everyone all day. Don't forget we need to pick up Hamlet from Tilly and Lana's today."

Kissing me on the nose, he murmurs, "I'm going to hop in the shower, care to join me?"

"When do you ever ask?"

"I was trying to be a gentleman to my fiancé, but you're right. I don't ask." In one swoop, I am heaved over Blake's shoulder and carried into the shower. Our laughter soon turns to seriousness as he kisses and caresses my body under the hot waterfall shower. This man, this now fiancé of mine, turns me completely inside out in the most sensual way.

I slipped into one of four sundresses I actually own that stay in Blake's closest. The dress is white with blue and gold threading for an outline. Leaving my hair down, I do full makeup, even a light gold eyeshadow to pop with the dress. I love his parents, but I always feel out of my comfy zone when we're with them. Especially at their home, which is a mansion for the mansions.

"Deep breaths, Amity. They already love you, and now with the past behind us, we only have our future to look forward to."

I sigh, shaking my head. "I know, but still. My nerves are sporadically firing off through my body with all the excitement from this morning. I'm just trying to wrap my hand around the fact this morning I was convinced I was going to lose you, and now, we are engaged, then everything in between. Plus, I always feel like I'm going to break something at your parents' house."

He laughs at me. "Baby," Laying his palms on my upper arms in support, he murmurs, "You do always break something."

My jaw drops. "You are such an ass!"

"I'm just speaking the truth. Besides, Mother has plastic dishes to use today, and all breakable art has been put away."

My eyes go wide. "Please tell me you are fuckin' joking, Blake."

He deadpans me, then waltzes off to the front door. "Let's go, my love. Our next adventure awaits." Huffing, I follow behind, still trying to figure out if he is messing with me or not.

I'm silent in the car and don't pay much attention to the four stops we seem to make on the way to his parents' house. He never gets back in the car with anything, nor does he put stuff in the trunk of his Corvette. Not like much would fit. I feel like I am only six inches off the ground in this sports car, but I will admit, this fancy car is fast as hell, and I love it when the top is down on a back road with Blake flooring the gas. When we finally drive up the windy driveaway to the front of the house, I begin to take deep breaths. "We need to call my parents as soon as we leave here, Blake. I can't let them think they were the last to know."

"Understood." Placing a kiss on my cheek, he gets out of the car, jogging to my side and opening my door. Taking my hand in his, he pulls out of the seat. "I got you, Amity. You and me." I wrap my hands around his forearms and lean my head into his chest. Even with heels on, I don't make the height to his face.

"Thank you."

Before we even make it to the front porch, the door swings open with his mom rushing to Blake and me for a tight hug. "I am so happy you two are back together." Then turning directly to me, she sniffles. "My beautiful darling, Amity. The daughter I never had."

"Mother! As much as I love your favoritism, don't say it so loud where others can hear. You do have a daughter-in-law."

Her carefree laugh echoes through the openness. "O honey, I love Willa, but I see so much of myself in Amity and the feisty-ness."

Now Blake laughs. "Shit. I should have thought about that beforehand." I punch him in his upper arm. "Ow, that actually hurt."

"Well good, next time I'll punch you even lower," I say with a smirk. Walking off arm and arm with his mother, we leave him there in exasperation. Soon, he is nipping at my heels, tugging my hair just enough to annoy me. Such a damn kid.

We stroll into the foyer, and Mrs. Holdings pulls me straight into the kitchen and then the back porch. I am shocked to find all my people gathered in the backyard. My mom and deddy are here next to Mr. Holdings. Willa, Nash, even her parents and brother, Dirks. I don't miss the fact that Dirks is standing close to Tilly. Then Lana and the third Holdings brother, Clint. Around the corner comes a running Hamlet, followed by Blake. I bend down to give him cuddles when I notice his blue collar has been switched out to a silver ribbon tied in a bow around his neck. Adorning a huge sparkling oval diamond ring. I gasp, putting my hand over my mouth in shock. This opens up the space for Hamlet to topple me over, and I go falling backwards on my ass, knocking over one of the Holdings' large flower cement planters.

Blake's dad shouts, "I win!" and with the commotion, I realize they were betting how long it would take for me to break something.

Tilly spills out, "I still think I am going to win the bet on her getting lost."

"Seriously, y'all!" Blake rushes to my side and bends down next to me. "Just ignore them." Untying the bow from Hamlet, he slides the ring off the ribbon into his hand. "This is not how I pictured this going, but what can I say? This is us." He pauses, palms sweaty. "This was so much easier this morning with just us. But in front of our friends and family, I ask you, Amity Jean Mercer, to be my wife. *Again*." His face when he says it sends me into a schoolgirl giggle, while the others laugh too. He reaches over to help pull me up, so we are standing facing each other. "I know I don't deserve you, but I will spend my entire life trying to be worthy of you." I swear only this man can make me cry.

Tears streaming down my face, I nod my head yes and fly into his arms to hold and kiss him. "I love you," I whisper in his ear, before he pushes me back a little so he can place the ring on my finger. "Um, Blake, this is way too much."

Nash shouts out, "Tell him, Amity. He didn't think it was big enough." Everyone goes into a fit of laughter. Blake shakes his head in annoyance but loves the attention.

"Because I know you so well, I also have this one for you." He presents me with a platinum band with a single small diamond embedded in the middle. "When you are riding, bar fighting, swimming, whatever trouble you are getting into, feel free to wear either or both." Before he places the second ring on my hand, he holds the ring up to my eyes, so I can see the engraving. I open my mouth to say the words, but he beats me to it. "You and Me. Always to Infinity."

"It's perfect," I say in awe, and he slips this one in front of the giant rock. Squeezing his face in between my hands, I pull him down to kiss me. Stepping back from him, I raise a brow. "Seriously though, how the hell did you plan all this in such a short notice?"

Willa walks up to me with a snort. "Short notice for you, not for the rest of us." She gives me her perfect smile and pulls me in for a hug. "I am so happy for you, and we are officially going to be a family. How exciting!" she squeals.

My eyes are wide, still in shock that this was planned before this morning. When I thought he was going off a whim. This means so much more, because this proves no matter my past, he always wanted to be with me.

"Mark this in the calendar, Amity is speechless!" Tilly shouts, running over to hug me, causing everyone to laugh. Then I am hugging a crying Lana, followed by my parents, Willa's family, then Blake's. I seriously need to get my shit together and stop crying. This is ridiculous.

"Alright you two, let me grab an engagement picture to share the news with," Mrs. Holdings tells us. Blake and I pose for a few underneath the large oak that resides in their backyard surrounded by colorful flowers. I think my favorite is Blake holding me piggy-back with my hand out in front showing off my new rings, because we are both laughing so hard, and the picture is genuine. Looks like us. After we do a few together, Mrs. Holdings insists on family photos, including Hamlet of course.

Once we have finished photos, and my soon to be mother in law has all the shots she can imagine, we finally sit down at the large wooden patio table for lunch with actual plastic dishes. Lunch was loud and delicious with juicy brisket and all the BBQ sides of potato salad, deviled eggs, garlic Texas toast, green beans, and hushpuppies. I'm stuffed and content. If this is what true happiness feels like, I never want to lose this feeling. I'm honestly not sure if I would survive losing any of this.

Blake leans over to kiss my cheek. "You look blissful."

"Because I am." Nudging his shoulder with my own, I grin. "Thanks to you." I'm then gifted with his sultry smile that makes my lower inside burn and ache.

Tilly interrupts my wicked thoughts over Blake with, "So, now for the most important question. When is the wedding?"

My mama claps her hands in excitement. "Yes, do tell!"

"Y'all! This just went down a few hours ago. I have no clue." I turn to look at Blake, sensing his overexcitement.

"I say next month," he spits out, making every gasp in surprise and me looking at him dumbfounded.

"You can't plan a wedding in a month, Blake," his mother says in shock.

"You aren't even home, man. Don't forget you have Brazil for the next three months. The deal was Clint would step in once you deliver on the deals," Nash states to Blake, and he nods in understanding.

Turning to me, his lips turn down in a frown. "Sorry, babe," he whispers quietly, and I can feel the disappointment he exudes of still having to travel.

Looking out to everyone, I throw my hands up. "Can't we just elope, then have a big party?"

"Certainly not!" both our mom's shout.

"You are my only daughter, Amity. And don't you play the card we have been here before, because we haven't. Not like this. Not with your person. You can go all Annie Oakley you want, but I'll be damned if you don't put on a white dress and walk down that aisle with us there for you."

"Exactly. Blake is my youngest son. My little boy. Surely you two would not deprive a mother of watching her baby boy get married to the daughter I can't wait to call my own." All I can do is shrug my shoulders, knowing I was beaten down with a Thor's mallet on that option.

Blake speaks up again. "Okay, December. That gives you women four months to plan. I'll be back in the states full time by then and can help. The weather should be warm and all extended family is in and out of town anyhow that month, so it just makes sense." Everyone agrees and realizes this wedding is for all of them. My people, my family. For Blake, who I already know is going to be a Groom-zilla and make sure all wedding related things are over the top. I am just going to sit back and let them all do all the planning, and they can tell me when and where to show up.

By the time Blake and I leave, the date is picked, venue signed off on, wedding party selected, along with colors and theme. Lana has been assigned as my wedding planner, splitting her role as a bridesmaid with Tilly as my maid of honor, and Willa as my matron of honor. Plus, I was told I will be given a spreadsheet and calendar tomorrow of dates for upcoming wedding festivities.

Blake and I slide into the car, we both take a deep breath. "You sure you are ready for all this?" I ask without turning to him.

He quickly curls his fingers around my chin, pulling me to face him. "Marrying you, fuck yes. What just transpired there… I was honestly not prepared." We laugh then sweetly kiss. "Mmmmm," he groans against my lips. "Can't wait to get you home."

"Don't forget Lana is following us back to drop Hamlet off. He sighs with a sad puppy face which sends me into a fit of laughter. "Don't worry, she won't stay long. She has a wedding to plan in four months."

"Good. Because I'm going to devour you as soon as we walk through the door." He takes off down the driveway and onto the main road, us holding hands with him staring at the road and me looking to a future I never thought was possible.

CHAPTER 11:
BLAKE

I'm home for two more days before flying back to Brazil for two weeks and then back for four days, then to do all over again for the next three months. Today I have lived my life on the phone, tightening up proposals and ensuring the men we need to persuade are having a splendid time. We came over to Amity's this morning due to needing clothes before going to work this morning and decided to stay here for the remainder of the days. Looking down at my watch, I notice it is four in the afternoon already. Amity should be back soon, so maybe I can be nice and start dinner for us. I know I personally haven't eaten all day with the workload piling up.

Hamlet follows me into the kitchen and starts to bark at his bowl. He must be hungry. "O shit, Ham. Did you not get breakfast?" He sits and glares with a light growl surfacing to barking. "Alright, alright, lets go get you some food." Once fed, he settles down, and I go about pulling pork chops and vegetables out of the fridge. I am chopping up vegetables when Hamlet starts barking at the door, and then I hear him jumping up and down in excitement when Amity walks through the door. With my back turned, focusing on the frying pan,I call out, "My girl is finally home."

Silence.

I slowly turn my head to look over my shoulder to be met with stern face Amity. *Fuuucck, what did I do now?*

Racking my brain, I take the road to not speak at all and possibly implicate myself further. Giving her my sultry smile, I turn back to flip the pork chops and toss onions into the pan. More silence, and a hole is being burned into the back of my scalp. I remove the food from the pan then walk back over to the fridge to grab a chilled bottle of wine. I turn to look at her just in time to duck as a small vase flies toward my head. "What the actual fuck, Amity?" Glaring at her, I'm tempted to throw the wine bottle back at her.

She chunks a rolled-up magazine toward my chest, which I let fall to the ground. "Are you done throwing shit at me?" Her arms cross over her chest with her ice daggers ready to soar to kill me.

"Go ahead, pick up the magazine." She is daring me to, but my stubborn ass refuses, glaring back at her. "You stubborn horse's ass!" Stalking toward me, I step back a bit. She leans down to pick it up off the floor, then unravels it, holding the front cover in my face. My eyes widen at the site of the cover of Texas Monthly, but then grin with the beauty of the cover.

"You knew this was going to happen. I'm confused as to why your panties are in a wad over this."

"Seriously, Blake. A damn heads up would have been much appreciated. How the hell did this even get pushed through at the last minute? I have been dodging questions and autographing most of my day. Spent two of my classes in the breakroom with the door locked because my colleagues were just as crazy as my students over this news."

"You know my mother knows people. Plus this was huge news." Reading the title of the cover, I don't see what's wrong with it. "Casanova Holdings is OFF the Market! Congratulations Blake and Amity. Open to page 264 for details and who is this mystery woman that stole the heart of Texas's beloved playboy." All this with one of the pictures my mother had taken yesterday at lunch.

"I might kill you myself," she grits out.

Stepping towards her, I lift my hands in surrender. "Baby, if I would have known, I would have given you the heads up. I have not heard from anyone all day."

"Whatever. Over it now," she pouts, turning to walk away from me, but I grip her wrist, twirling her back into me then trapping her between my body and countertop. "You don't get to turn away from me, Amity. You especially do not get to leave me still pissed off."

"Not mad," she mutters, avoiding eye contact. I wrench her wrists in my one hand, while my left hand grabs her chin to push it up.

"Look at me Amity." She hesitates, but then her ice daggers pierce my soul. "We can play this game all night if you want." Her eyes shift away from mine, pushing me to grab her attention again. With her face still locked in my hand, I lick up her cheek, gliding my tongue down her neck before biting and nipping along her collarbone. A painful hiss escapes between her gritted teeth. "Don't resist me, baby. You want me, right here right now, don't you?" Locking eyes with hers, I lean down to subtly kiss her plump lips, only for her to suck my bottom lip in, then bite down, drawing blood. Pulling back and licking my bottom lip, tasting the sweet iron sends a rage through me. I rotate her body, pushing her top half into the counter.

Using one hand, I'm holding her wrists behind her in one swoop of motion. With my other hand, I yank her skirt down with her panties, leaving them to pool at her feet. Then I quickly undo my buckle and pants, pushing them down to my knees. "Someone wants to play dirty tonight," I whisper in her ear. Sliding my hand down her backside until I reach her heat, I pull back for a moment. *Slap.* Amity lets out a groan, but I can tell she is still holding back from enjoying herself. I push and circle her nub, pulling squeaks out of her, then slap her pussy again. "Wet. So wet for me, my beautiful princess. Indulge yourself in the pleasure and pain. Give in to me, Amity." I push the tip of my cock into her soaked folds, taunting her. "Tell me you want me, you stubborn woman," I hiss, pushing my long shaft into her sweet heat, only to pull back out when she moans. I repeat the act several more times, knowing I'm pushing her over the edge when she pushes her ass into me. Lifting her top half off the counter, I take her shirt off with no protest. Unsnap her bra, letting it fall to the floor. Groping her perky breasts in my palms, I squeeze and fondle them roughly in between pulling her mouth back to mine to kiss her. I have her where I want her when she spins around, wrapping her hand around my cock.

"I don't like you at this moment, but you need to fuck my cunt right now or I'll handle my own pleasure."

"I love when you talk dirty to me," I purr, picking her up and wrapping her legs around my waist. I shuffle to the kitchen table and lay her down, quickly pulling my pants off then I'm crawling over her on top of the table.

"We are going to break the table," she giggles out.

"I'll buy a new one," groaning, pushing myself firmly inside her. Her back arches off the table with a loud moan. Then we find ourselves in a perfect rhythm. "Fuck me. You are a goddess with your tight pussy." She then swivels her hips against me causing me to release a deeply throated growl.

"Blake!" is shouted from her intoxicating mouth which unravels me. Pulsing inside her while she milks me dry is the second best feeling in the world. First, is just being near her, touching her. Third, is, of course, when her mouth is wrapped around my length. She relaxes underneath me.

"You good now?" I ask, arching my eyebrow.

"I am, thank you." Leaning up kissing me on the cheek. "I love you, Blake Holdings," she says with a smile, sauntering off to the bedroom. Just like that, there is peace in our world again, thanks to an orgasm.

CHAPTER 12:
MONTH 1

We are coming to the end of month one of being engaged and Blake hating his travel schedule. I see him every other week for a four-day weekend. In reality, it is only 3 days when we take into account the travel time. I can tell he is exhausted from working extra-long hours and keeping up with everything at home. Honestly, if he is still standing by the end of this, I will be impressed. His assistant Ross has my number on speed-dial now after an incident two weeks ago. I felt awful for Ross having to witness the side of Blake people fear.

Apparently, an investor was looking to pull out right when the particular deal was being signed, which then caused other investors to question the land they would be drilling on. Between Clint and Blake, they have never been wrong on where oil is found. They have a crazy sixth sense for oil on top of all the research and testing they do before bringing the land to the table to drill on. After punching one of the older guys, breaking his nose, and another walked away with a few broken ribs, Blake played his cards of knowing who was having affairs, connections to smugglers, and even those who spank their assistants. He had them all blackmailed for one reason or another. To top all the bullshit off, Blake raised the investment cost just to prove his point of not to be fucked with. I'm not sure I will ever get over the fact that the man I love can be a ruthless businessman. Huh, I guess this proves I have a type. At least this one won't cut me up and torture my family. **#*winning.***

Thanks to Lana, we have to fit in cake tasting this weekend. I opted for a tower of Shipley's Do-nuts. Still pushing for it, but Groom-zilla sides with Lana on why we need a traditional cake. Between Blake and Lana, they practically have the whole wedding organized and planned down to table placements, food, and having his old Pastor booked to perform the ceremony. The only thing I have been asked to approve of were the wedding invitations. Luckily, I went with instinct on what I knew Blake would prefer. Tying our tastes together. Rustic Lace invitations that have a country feel, but expensive and extravagant to fit Blake. I did deny him his grooms' cake of a bloody Armadillo. Secretly his favorite movie is Steel Magnolias and thought he would follow suit with a replica. Finally mortified, Lana and I both were able to convince him otherwise, but is now keeping a secret of what he decided on. Like I have said before, this man of mine hates being vetoed. Revenge is in my future. I'm sure of it.

Right now, I am leaving school to head to Crenshaw Ranch for dinner tonight. Blake is meeting me there plus the rest of the group for a large steak-out. Literally grilling the best cut of meat, you can find in these parts. Right off my parents' ranch. My parents have supplied their beef for the last four years to the Crenshaw Ranch, and tonight, we are celebrating their beef getting picked up by the Albertsons chain and a handful of local grocery stores. I drive by Carter's's Calvin Klein billboard and think how not long ago, my future looked so much different. He has even called a few times to check in and plan another "get" together. Of course, I declined and told him to check with Blake. Honestly though, the thought of bedding several others besides my soon-to-be husband no longer interests me. He gives me all I need. The temptation, the pain, the power, and all the pleasure. Not saying it won't change down the road and to keep things interesting, but right now, he is all I need in all aspects of my life.

Driving down the ranch's driveway, I see one of the longhorns have escaped by breaking through the fence. That damn bastard. He's a mean son of a bitch too. Texting Willa that I am stopping to try and push him back in, to bring help and tools, I get out and begin the standoff away from my truck. He put a hole in Dirks' truck not long ago when Dirks was driving across the pasture then stopping to throw some fresh cattle feed out.

"Alright Jetson, let's move!" I shout, waving my arms in the air to catch his attention. For a hot second, I'm in awe of how quick and graceful he moves. Only to remember he is heading in my direction, so I take off running down the path until I see the opening in the fence.

Jetson follows me back into the pasture just as Willa and Dirks drive up. Dirks works quickly to fix the fence while Willa is game planning on how to get me out of this situation since Jetson is blocking my line to freedom. My other option is to jump the fence behind me where Leroy is. Leroy is the kindest longhorn, but I don't want to risk Jetson barging through that part of the fence and start a legit bull fight. An idea hits me that if I jump on one of my female longhorns, I might be able to outrun him to the fence. I shout to Willa my game plan, just as Jetson finishes stomping his hoof and on his way to me. I barely have time to notice the Uber pulling in and stopping to watch the show. As soon as my ass lands on Clover's back, she takes off. Takes off in the wrong direction, with Jetson hot on her hoofs. Willa and Dirks jump over to catch Jetson's attention. That is when I spot Blake standing there in his expensive tailored suit, looking gorgeous but pissed off while his hands rest on his hips. Knowing I need to dip off sooner than later to save Clover from getting hurt, I quickly steer her by her loose neck to the water trough. Right when she passes, I let myself fall in. By the grace of God, my body hits the water with my feet out. I sit up, coughing up water, pushing the hair out of my face, to face an angry Jetson. Luckily for me, his horns are as long as the trough, but he keeps punching my arm with his nose.

"What is it, man? Do you need to get laid?" I snort just as he sneezes, sending hay and green snot into my face. Using my country napkin, I wipe my face off. "Thanks, Jetson." I slowly reach my hand out to pet his nose, and surprisingly he lets me. Until I hear Blake shouting my name like I am about to be murdered. Jetson starts to scoff his hoof again, which tells me someone else has entered his pasture. Turning around, I'm stunned with Blake running toward me. Dirks hot on his heels. I turn back to Jetson just in time to duck from his swinging horns because now he is pissed off again. I quickly jump out of the trough and haul ass to Blake and Dirks, telling them to run. Like RUN! Ever seen the scene from Jurassic Park when Dr. Sattler pisses off the velociraptors and tries to escape them as her rescuers run to her? This is what this scene looks like, except a very large, angry longhorn with several of his female companions stampeding behind him.

Before I know it, I am tossed over the fence into Blake's arms, and we help pull Dirks over at the last minute. Willa barreling on the ground laughing as she recorded the whole scene. Jetson and the others stopped right at the fence, huffing at us. Right then, Mr. Crenshaw drives up with Ben. "Time to set up the electric fence. Not sure it will do much for that son of a bitch, but we can try."

Still breathing heavily, I let a laugh slip out. Blake glares at me. "This is not funny, Amity. What if something happened to you?"

"Nothing did, pretty boy. I'm fine," I say with a grin. Could that have gone really sideways? Of course. But hell, I'm still in one piece, so all good. Willa comes over to help me up and hug me.

"For the love of Zeus, Am." All I can do is nod my head. "Still, I can't believe he let you pet him!" she squeals.

"Right. I thought I was getting somewhere with him." Blake stalks off to my truck, slamming the door on the passenger side. "Let me go deal with Diva-Bitch. He must be thinking he won't have a bride for this extravagant wedding."

Willa lets out a chuckle. "You are awful. Go thank him for saving your life because that's what he needs to hear."

"Because I am the perfect gal to stroke a man's ego?" I ask, looking at her questionably with my eyebrow cocked.

She laughs again. "Just go be sweet, Amity. Then get y'alls ass washed up for dinner. I'll bring some dry clothes to the eatery for you." Nodding my head, I head back to my truck.

I take a deep breath, before I open the door and climb up. Once in, I start my truck, then turn to look at him. "Thank you for helping me out back there."

Without evening turning to look at me, he grumbles, "You're welcome."

"Blake, I am fine, we are all fine. It was just an adventure. I rodeo for a living and have fallen off plenty while ropn'n and bucked off steers and broncs. Something crazy is always bound to happen when dealing with these animals. But all this is part of my livelihood. Part of me." I pause for him to say something.

"I think my heart stopped when you fell into the trough, but then started again when I saw you reach your hand out to pet him. Because you are a crazy ass woman, Amity. I started running in your direction because my next fear was you were going to try and ride him." He doesn't even blink his crystal baby blue eyes while glaring at me.

"I will never ride Jetson, I promise. Leroy on the other hand, he is a big teddy bear, but not Jetson," I promise through a laugh.

"Like that is much better, Amity."

"Ugh, come on. You know we can laugh about this now, and you know your soon to be wife is a complete cowgirl and badass, so let's move on." I scooch over, placing a soft kiss on his cheek.

Right when I fall back, Blake's hand goes up into my hair, tightening around the bottom of my neck. "Mine," he growls out. "Through the heaven gates or fiery pits of hell, I will always find you and keep you safe." Our eyes locking, I go in for his lips. He believes his words with his whole being, and so do I. My halo is already bent, so lord knows I need all the extra saving I can get. Our kiss turns feverishly passionate, and before I know it, I am straddling him on the bench seat of my truck. Grinding against him. I look around to find everyone else has turned back to the house, leaving him and I alone. My clothes and body are already soaked, but I can feel the warm wetness leaking out of my core just for him. I can feel him swelling in his suit pants for me, so I reach down to undo his belt and pants, pulling them down just enough to free him. "I need you now," he whispers in my ear, gripping my hair tightly. I could come on the spot listening to his sensual voice that feels like velvet wrapping around my body. I roll off him just to get my boots, panties, and pants off, then straddle him again. Slicking his shaft with my wetness. "Fuck, take me now, Amity."

I hear another truck come down the drive. *Damn.* As much as my body needs him, I know we are running late to dinner and putting on a scene for anyone driving by to see. My voyeur amusement draws the line at family. Rolling off him, slipping my panties back on, I murmur, "Will have to wait till later, cowboy. I promise I'll ride you hard and fast." Kissing him on the cheek, Blake remains frozen in disbelief.

"I think that is the cruelest action you have taken against me."

"Don't take it personally. We just have somewhere else to be. A place where all our family and friends are." Blake huffs, pulling his suit pants back up while I drive us down the road. A promise kept; Willa runs off the porch of the eatery to bring me some dry clothes. Once dressed, we jump out of the truck and join the party. Ain't no better smell than fresh steaks grilling, wafting in the light breeze of an early fall evening.

CHAPTER 13:
MONTH 2

Week three of month two. *Calgary take me away.* This time of the year is busy without the added stress of a wedding, sexual frustration, and time management. A million and one issues have occurred for Blake and the Holdings company, causing him to miss his last two visits home, along with the brothers headed down to Brazil for a week. Someone has managed to hack their system, leaking pieces of information. Not that they have anything to hide, but clients want their information protected, as we all do. Last I heard, they tracked down the source and were given over to Blake and Clint for questioning before they pull the authorities in. Me, I am trying to push through mid-semester finals, plus grading on top of getting my top ten students placed for internships to start two months.

I have tried to help Lana with wedding planning, because I know how buried Blake is right now, but shit. She has me picking out placement cards, completing guest lists and seating arrangements. I'm still wishing Blake would just come home and whisk me off to Vegas. Matrimony under neon lights and with Elvis is my type of wedding. Not all of this. Doesn't help Groom-zilla has me running over all the updates at night with him, and then he ends up making several more changes I then have to relay to Lana. I am on a vicious ride between the two of them. Luckily Blake is to be home tomorrow evening for a few days, so he can take over for the time being.

I'm walking up to my apartment when I notice a bouquet of wildflowers by my front door. Just then my phone rings, and I see it's Blake. "Hey you."

"Hey princess. Just getting home?"

After unlocking my door, I pick up the vase of flowers and walk in. "I am. You sound exhausted." Setting the flowers on the counter, while he answers me.

"I am, but no worries. Soon enough, I'll be back with you and can breathe a little for a few days."

"Say hi, Hamlet." He lets out a deep bark, getting a chuckle out of Blake, who says hi back.

"Glad to hear you are still coming. I thought you sent these flowers to say you're sorry," I say, laughing as he hates when I tease him.

"I think your secret admirer must have sent you those flowers. You know I'd prefer to surprise you with my dick in a box then flowers."

A slight laugh releases from me as my curiosity peaks. Putting the phone down on the counter and putting Blake on speaker, I go in search of a card. "Found the card, let's see who it could be." I open the envelope, slipping the little one-sided card into my hand. Flipping it over, I feel the blood rush from my face.

"Hello? Amity, you still there?" I gasp in shock, reading back over the written message. I would recognize that handwriting anywhere. "Babe. I can hear you breathing heavily. What is it?"

All I can mutter out is, "Gage."

"Did you say Gage?"

"Y..ye..yes."

"What does the card say?" he asks, but I'm unable to make actual thoughts, let alone words. I can't breathe, and the walls are closing in on me as I sink to the floor.

BLAKE

I have never felt more useless than in the last five minutes. I hung up on Amity to call Willa for her to get her ass to Amity's. She conferences in Tilly and Lana so they are aware and to figure out who can get to her the fastest. I have all three on the way, with Lana ahead of them being only ten minutes out. Then I call Nash to have him get security over to her apartment. My fingers keep dialing Amity back, with no answer. Clint is luckily still with me in Brazil, so I loop him in, and now I am heading to the runway to board our plane home. I'm not leaving her there without me for another twelve plus hours. Phone rings, and I hastily pick it up. "Hey Nash, any update?"

"Police are on their way with two of our security guards. They are going to stay with her until you get back. Then we can decide the next course of action."

"Thanks. I'm headed to the runway now. Clint has everything under control. We had all our meetings this morning, plus we turned the source over to the authorities. It was going to take near murdering him to get answers, but I know we needed to turn him over."

"What a fucking mess this all is. Right now just get home to your girl, and I'll meet you over there. I'm actually headed over there now to meet Willa and see what we can turn up."

"I owe you one."

"Nah, you don't. You have helped a million times over with Willa, plus we are brothers. Apparently in love with women who know how to find trouble." I laugh because of the immense truth of that one statement.

"Alright, Lana is beeping in, so let me take this." We say bye, and I click over. "Are you there?"

"About to walk in but wanted you on the phone just in case someone else is around." My sympathy sits with Lana. She had a shitty fiancé that I think did more damage to her then she lets on, on top of that, I just tossed her into a possible Lion's Den. Maybe we should have waited until the cops showed up. Fuck that, I need to know Amity is there and fine.

"O poor sweetie," I hear Lana say. "She is curled up on the floor with Hamlet in shock. Let me see if I can get her up." Lana puts the phone down on the floor, and all I can do is listen in on their conversation. "Amity, can you sit up with me?"

"Just leave me here. He has found me. It's only a matter of time."

"A matter of time until what? He let you go, Amity. Do you think he would come back and hurt you?" I hear exasperated sobs escape Amity, causing my heart to crack. "O sweetie, he won't. Come on, let's get you off the floor and onto the couch." Hamlet's paws clicking on the tile lets me know they are on the move.

"Hello?"

"Hey Tilly."

"Willa is almost here."

"Okay good. Can you grab her a glass of water?"

"Yeah." Footsteps walk by the phone. "How is she?"

"In shock. Worried he is coming for her."

"Hello!" I shout through the phone.

"Snapples! I forgot I had Blake on the phone. Can you grab it?"

"Hey, it's Tilly."

"I figured. Can you Facetime her so I can talk to her?" She flips to facetime, facing me to a pale, scared, and shocked Amity. "Baby, you listening?" She nods her head yes. "I'm headed to you. Ten minutes from getting on a plane. Nash is headed there with security and the police. I want you to either stay at my place tonight or you go with the girls. Okay?" She nods again. "I love you, and that man will not be getting anywhere near you. I will kill him with my bare hands if he tries." She blinks more tears away. "Tell me you understand. Use your words."

"Yes, I understand."

"Tell me you love me and trust me."

She sighs in annoyance, which lets me know she is going okay. "I love you and trust you, Blake."

"Good. Now hand the phone back to Tilly."

"Tilly, take me off speaker."

"You're off."

"Show me the card." Once in view, I take a screenshot. "Okay. I just pulled in. Call me if anything changes and make sure she gets out of there tonight. Once the police come, throw the flowers away and give the card to Nash."

"On it. Just get home safely. We have her until then."

"Thank you," I slowly say before hanging up.

Once the plane took off, I ordered six bourbon shots. Downed them all to fight the edge of losing control. Now I am staring at my phone, reading the message over and over again.

My Dearest Amity,

Did you think I was gone for good? Did you not think I would not find out about your engagement? You silly girl.

I guess you finally stopped looking behind you, but I haven't stopped watching you. I've had years to think about you, about us. Time has healed all my wounds except the ones that are seared into my memory of you. I'm coming for you, because you have always been mine to have. I've let you have your fun, renew yourself, waiting to strike. I guess the time has come.

Because over your dead body, will you marry another.

See you soon, my wildflower.

A coldness washes over me with knowledge that I will need to find this man and kill him myself. Nash told me a while ago, he was in El Paso. Now I'm unsure if I need to start there or look closer to home for him. Our worlds have never crossed, but I am about to go under siege and send him to meet his maker.

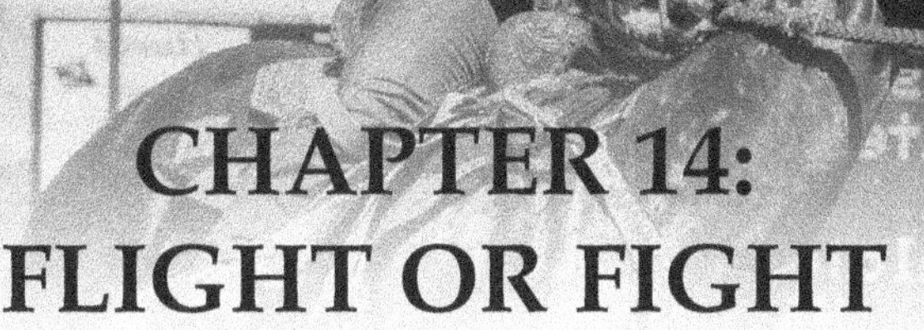

CHAPTER 14:
FLIGHT OR FIGHT

I'm two days in post-shock of Gage reaching out. Blake has been a saint, dealing with my rollercoaster of emotions. I feel so angry at Gage, furious at myself for letting my guard down, and scared to death of what he might do because I know what he is capable of. Fearing what he could do to those closest to me, just to get to me. I put nothing past the man I once knew, even more so to what he could have become. Right now, I'm hunkered down at Blake's apartment with guards at the door. Knowing tomorrow, I need to leave here and go on with my life, with my job without fear. With fear, he already has a hold on me. Something I refuse to immerse myself in. I have guards that will be following my every move, plus Blake who is determined to be at school with me all week. He is also working with Nash to track Gage down. Bringing in all the top-tier people they know to help find him.

I've asked to cancel or move the wedding with no avail. If anything, Blake is thinking of moving it up to throw everyone off and make it more intimate. I told him I will not be in a mindset to marry until I know we are all safe. I will marry him when I no longer feel like my life has been violated and unhinged. For him, he is determined to murder him. Blake's recent demeanor has been more intense than I could have imagined. I have always known he has a devilish side, but recently, I could swear his baby blues are coated in blood red. Murder is the only course of action he deems acceptable. I, of course, just want him gone, but not by Blake's hands or by anyone else I know. I'm not sure that I can live with that when all is said and done.

The past two weeks have been quiet. I leave the apartment with Blake, go straight to school, followed by bodyguards, then come straight home afterwards. No going out to eat or to the bar with my girls. They, of course, are wonderful and bring the bar life to me for a few hours. I've not even been back to the ranch, which I think is worse than missing all the other usual activities. Blake said maybe we can go out on Sunday, so I can at least visit and ride Nevada. He can sense me snapping soon, and then all hell will break loose.

Today we pull up to my apartment so I can check the mail and grab a few items. I wasn't worried walking into my apartment as no damage was actually done, plus I have Mutant one and two going ahead of me. They exude Blake's madman personality on steroids. When I walk in, I realize I miss my space, but then I look over at my coffee table where there is a vase filled with at least two dozen yellow roses.

"What the fuck?" I hear Blake say, coming up behind me. He beats me to them, opening the card. "My dearest, Amity, Maybe I was too blunt last time, which caused you to run with your tail between your legs. Don't worry though, I know where you are and where you go. Tell your boy toy to back off, before I bring his whole company down. On another note, please enjoy the flowers per an act of friendship. Because maybe that is where we need to start after all this time. In time, I am sure you will love me again. See you soon, my wildflower." Blake reads the note out loud, and for the life of me, I can't fathom how they even got inside without security catching him or his lackey.

Blake is on the phone in an instant. "Nash, I know who is sabotaging us…" Fucking Gage. "I have all the proof we need in a card he sent Amity…yes, fuck, he sent more." He kicks the ottoman, sending it flying across the room. Turning to my left, I spot Mutant one on the phone with the detective on my case. I sink to the couch, curling up into a ball, as those around me handle the shit show that has become my life.

BLAKE

I'm at a loss for words right now. Amity is crawling the walls already, and now this bullshit. We have several leads on Gage's whereabouts, but every time we get close, he moves. As much as I prefer his blood on my hands to know he is done for, I know in my heart Amity would never look at me the same. I need to find him and turn him over. Detective Barge has talked to me about setting a trap to lure him out with Amity as bait. Up till now, that has been a hard no from me. Now that idea might be worthwhile. Only if I can guarantee her safety.

Rocking on my heels in my home office, I call him to discuss the details. By the time we have run through the plan for the tenth time, it seems solid. The kicker is, Amity can't know she is bait. We can't take the chance of her body language to show something array. Plus, I have to talk

Nash into letting Willa take her out to the bar and be involved unknowingly also. I run my palm down my face then fist my hair in both hands. I've been trying with all my means to be strong for Amity. To keep my own fears in check, but this shit is real. She thought I was crazy for letting loose on her after the bull incident. That was child's play compared to what I'm fucking feeling right now. I need to be her rock, her protector.

I've kept away from being sexual and intimate with her, fear of what might shake up in her or even my own self. Like I'm worried to even let my guard down enough in fear of breaking down in front of her or allowing Gage to wedge his way in. *Fuck! Maybe he already has.* Amity and I are living like college roommates right now with a dog. We barely talk, eat meals in silence, and sleep facing away from each other. Both of us unsure of what's to come but too stubborn to talk about any of it. This is where I need her to talk first. Set the boundary for me. Let me in to help her so I know what our next move is together.

The girls have been great coming around and so have her parents and mine. They bring food over and games to keep our minds off the looming predator. Of course, they are all covered with extra security. No one complains, and we are all taking this day by day. My girl though is a hard-ass as much as she is a badass, which is why it has been so hard to break her shield with all of this going on. She took forever to even open-up about her past, now two months later, she is faced with the nightmare again. Her screams are louder now while she sleeps. Waking in the morning drenched in sweat. I haven't slept in days watching over her. Whether I'm trying to wake her from her terror, or rock her back to sleep. Her blood curdling screams haunt my mind when I close my eyes. Visions of her being accosted by a sick man who claims he loves her. On top of that, the first week she binge ate, now I have to practically force feed her. Honestly, if she snaps, I'm a goner. There will be no pulling me out of the abyss until her life is safe. Even over my own.

CHAPTER 15:
MONTH 3

Two more deliveries of flowers have been sent since the last one. One to my school and the other to Blake's. The one to Blake's just so happened to be the week he was in Brazil tying up some loose ends with Clint before he can be back home officially. Once they found out Gage was behind hacking their system, they were able to get ahead of the problem and communicate with their clients. I pushed him to go. I needed the space. Hell, he needed the space and distraction just as much. The one sent to my school was a bouquet of a dozen red roses. The card was along the lines of Gage loving me and how he could not wait to roll my body across the thick thorned roses and watch me bleed as he took me for his own again. How touching I know.

The second was Lilies. This delivery represented what he will lay on my grave if I move forward with the wedding. That when he comes for me, I better be ready to let go of my life here. I remember his last sentence and can hear his edgy voice, "Time is soon, as I'm just around the corner. I can't wait for you to bleed for me Amity while I take you. This is you're last warning to leave Blake and never mention him in my presence again. Sincerely yours, my wildflower."

That one still sends a chill down my spine, and at the time, I panicked. Blake came home to me moved in with Tilly and Lana. I took Hamlet with me, leaving no trace of my existence but my hangers swinging in his closet.

In turn, sent him in a rage and wrecked his corvette into a guardrail that night. Luckily, he was fine, and he is now staying with Nash and Willa. I've already felt so distant from him over these past two months, some more time apart to keep him alive will be worth my own life. The world can't lose Blake. Every side of him is a gift, body, mind, and soul. He brightens the room when he walks in like the sun rising over the mountains. My past won't be his downfall. That is why I have already come up with a plan. Gage is waiting for the opportunity for me to be in the open, alone, and that is just what I am going to give him. I only wish I had one more night with Blake. To let him feel and be consumed by my love, but hopefully my letter will suffice for him.

Tilly and Lana won't be home for another hour, and what the guards don't know is I have it in me to jump from the second-floor balcony. I'll land in the bushes and be fine. By the time they realize something is amiss, I'll be hauling ass down the road in my truck.

Paramour has its grand re-opening tonight. The crowd is large, and the perfect place to be seen and hidden at the same time for someone looking. Gage will eventually find me; I'm counting on it. I've been here an hour already, and my phone has started blowing off the hook. Tilly and Lana are home and have found their letters. I let them in on my plan but did not enclose where I would be. I trusted them to let me follow through with my plan, so we could all live in peace again. I promised them that I would find my way back, but to give me this right now. To keep Blake at bay, but to help him move on if I don't come back. If this all ends tragically, because I feel the fear in my bones this could all end horribly. I turn my phone off and take a swig of my drink. Finding all the courage I need to get through this evening. Possibly longer.

Another hour goes by, and I have chatted with some acquaintances and past hookups. Smiling the whole time like I have no care in the world. All until the hot breath tickles the back of my neck, causing all the hair on my body to rise. "My beautiful wildflower," Gage whispers in my ear. I take a subtle breath then turn to face him. I'm met with his face leaned down to mine. His knuckles graze my cheek, and I let him.

"Looks like you finally found me."

"O my dearest, Amity, you were never lost to me. All this time, I knew exactly where you have been, who you've been with." He laughs like a mad man, and I know he truly became his father. "You truly are my gorgeous, tantalizing little slut, aren't you?" Taking my chin between his fingers. "I'm starting to think you enjoyed all those times I took you recklessly and uninvited. Here I was thinking for years of all the harm I caused you, only to see pictures of you in sex clubs being whipped or splayed out in bed with men and women devouring every inch of you. Maybe you were jealous when I had other women, because I wasn't including you when I was fucking them."

All I do is glare into his soulless brown eyes. "You broke me Gage," I grit out.

"Well then, wildflower, let me put you back together." Before I can speak, he drags me away from the bar, into one of the dimly lit corners of the roof. Pinning me between him and the wall. "You make me murderous in this dress, Amity. I wanted to kill every single person that looked your way this evening." Propping my leg up on his hip, while he slides his other hand up my thigh, under my dress. The touch of him makes me want to vomit, but I push through to see this play out. His fingers gently glide on the outside of my panties down my heat, causing him to groan and grind up against me. "Are you ready to come home with me?"

Looking up at him, I shrug. "I didn't think there was a choice in the matter."

"There isn't, but I would prefer you come willingly, rather than me carry you out of this club."

"Then yes, I'm ready."

His eyebrows furrow. "Are you playing me darling? You are coming too easily." Letting my leg down, he bulldozes my body into the wall.

"No game. I just want those I love safe."

An evil laugh escapes his lips. "Those you love, huh? Does that include Blake Holdings?"

"You told me not to speak of him, so I am not."

"Tell me you don't love him, Amity," he growls. I refuse to speak, because my mouth is incapable of saying those words. A scream flies out of my mouth when I realize Gage has bent down and bitten my upper arm.

"Holy fuck, Gage!"

"I see your mouth has gotten dirtier. I told you; you would bleed for me, Amity." His tongue slowly licks up my bleeding arm then he sucks where his teeth marks are, sending a painful burning sensation through my whole body. He pulls away, takes me by the arm. "Let's go, wildflower, we have a flight to catch."

BLAKE

"She did what? How the fuck did she get out with no one seeing her? I am going to murder her myself when I find her!" I shout, throwing my glass of scotch across the room, nearly missing Nash's head, but he moved before it shattered against the wall. I take survey of the room. Both families, our friends, and all the guards are here, plus Detective Barge. Nash had everyone come to his house once we learned Amity went missing. Our first instinct was she was taken by Gage. Only for Lana to spill the beans on Amity's escape plan that was to be kept secret.

"Calm down, man. We will find her." I give Nash the glare of his positive pattiness is not working tonight, and he needs to step away from me before I throw a punch. He heeds my warning and moves back.

"Does anyone have a clue where she could have gone? We have already checked at Howls, the school, airport, and bus station. Her phone is off, so I can't track her"

No one seems to know as the minutes tick by. *Ding! Ding!* We all look at Willa. She hurriedly tries to silence her phone then, "O shit," flies out of her mouth.

We all go "what?"

"The text is from Toby and Eric. They saw Amity leave Paramour with some man. They thought it was strange she was not with us or you and wanted to check on her to make sure she was okay… I'm so sorry Blake, I didn't even remember tonight was a grand reopening with all of this happening."

"Call them right now and tell them to stall. To follow. FUCK! Don't let her out of their sight." Grabbing my keys, we rush to our cars.

"Blake, get in the car with me," Detective Barge warns, and I do. He is already on the phone with dispatch to get his team over to Paramour. I call Nash, knowing he and the crew are behind us.

"Any update?"

"They saw her get into a black escalade with tinted windows. Followed by three others. No license plate, the cars all look unmarked."

I slam my fist into the dash. "Calm down there, diva. Don't go breaking my shit." I laugh.

"Amity calls me a diva bitch sometimes."

"Well hell, I can see why." He earns my icy glare as he calls back in to dispatch to block off all exits and roads leading to the highway from Paramour. "Even if they split up the vehicles to throw us off, we will trap them."

"I sure hope so," I murmur, then pray in my head just let my girl be safe.

CHAPTER 16:
SOMEONE ALWAYS DIES

I've already heard the communication amongst the driver and Gage that roads are starting to be blocked off. Part of me is pissed at my friends for not letting me see this through, but the other half knows I would have done the same damn thing. God loving pineapples, if I make it out of this alive, please let Blake forgive me. Gage is yelling at his driver to take certain turns to avoid barricades.

Then I hear him on the phone with someone else. "Frank, I need you to touchdown in the pasture at mile marker fifty-six. Sending you the coordinates now…I don't give a fuck about your license, you work for me asshole. The only person you should worry about pissing off is ME!" he screams, then hangs up, slamming his phone down on the seat.

"I can't believe I let some little bitch trick me into this shit." *Is he talking about me? He must be.* A punch to the arm, then slap across my face gives me confirmation. I dare not look his way or move to hold the throbbing pain in my upper arm or sting on my face. "I was so hell bent on getting to you, I lost sight of what you could be up to. Though my team was supposed to have all this handled in case your sneaky ass was up to no good."

"I swear, Gage, I did not try to pull one over on you. No one knew I left the house tonight. They must have contacted someone that might have seen me tonight."

"Too late now, wildflower, revenge will be mine once we get out of here."

"Please, no, Gage. Just let them all be. You have what you want."

"Do I? Do I really, Amity?" he asks condescendingly. From that point on, I knew both of us were in a race against time.

BLAKE

Took us over thirty minutes to get downtown and to Paramour in the midst of traffic and all the mess with the barricades. Two of the four escalades have been detained, but neither had Amity or willing to give up her whereabouts. When we pull into Paramour, I scan the parking lot for her black Duramax until I spot it. I rush over for any sign of a hint or just something I can grasp on to, to know she is okay. I quickly spot an envelope on her dash with my name written across it, followed by noticing she left her doors unlocked. Amity knew I would come for her sooner than later. I grab the letter and head back over to Detective Barge and crew.

"We have eyes in the sky on the last vehicles. We also got word that a helicopter with no flight plan is hovering over a field off Chamberlin Road."

"What the hell are we waiting for? That's for them. I know it." He gives me a pensive look but proceeds behind me to his car. Once in, I open the letter and read as he drives. Vomit gets stuck in the back of my throat as I read on.

Blake, I hope one day you find enough peace with all of this to forgive me. My promise to you during my absence is to fight like hell to return to you, but in the instance I never make it home, please know I did this for us, for you, for our friends and family. They all need you way more than my toxic self, and if giving Gage what he wants protects all those that I love, honestly, I could care less what happens to me. You made me see a brighter future full of love I thought I never deserved. So please do not come looking for me. Move on and pursue your best life without a thought toward me. I will be fine, I promise. In the event a year passes without my return, all my assets have been split equally amongst Willa, Tilly, Lana, my parents, and you. I've enclosed my lawyer's card to contact him when the time comes. Also, he will continue to pay for Nevada's board at the Crenshaw ranch. My utilities are cut off in my absence, but he will sell my apartment at the year mark as well. I've taken an extended leave from work with a temporary replacement, who can become permanent if needed. My rings are tucked away in an envelope in your nightstand. As you can sense now, I have been planning on this for a while.

I wish I could have been in your bed, made love to you, and fallen asleep in your arms one more time as these months have not been kind to us. But please know, you will always have my heart. No other has a heart like mine but you.

I love you.

Always and Infinity,

Amity

The notion that I have not sobbed since I was a little kid is not lost on me. Amity has completely shattered me, and I am unsure how to process these bittersweet emotions. To be so loved by someone they are willing to risk their own self, but to know you are obsessively in love with them to do the same. I feel a sharp punch to my arm. "What the hell?"

"I've been hollering your name for damn near five minutes, Blake. I need to know you're prepared for all hellfire as we are about to pull in." My eyes roll in the back of my head, dragging my palm roughly down my face. Reality settling in that I can still get my girl back. This isn't over until it's over. Opening the door to step out, I'm stopped. "Whoa, cowboy, meet me at the trunk before you take off and get yourself killed." I step out to see Nash and the girls behind him.

Detective tosses me a vest to put on. "Is this going to save me if he aims for my head?"

"You Holdings boys are a bunch of smartasses, aren't yah? No, it will not. Eight out of ten times in long range shots, the bullet will hit the region your vest covers, which is exactly where you will be. Away from the scene, but close enough I can keep an eye on yah."

"Whatever you say man, let's just get my girl back." He pats me on the back, and Nash gives me a salute. I take in the scene in front of me through the pitch black. There are several police cars lined up on the north side of the field, but everyone has their lights out, and we wait. Twenty minutes go by when we finally hear the helicopter coming from the backend to get closer to the road. Just then, an Escalade pulls up quickly, but they seem to take their time getting out. Before we know it, shots are firing behind us, and we all throw down for cover. My eyes never once left the SUV, and I soon see the driver walk around, opening the passenger side door. My heart stops once I see Amity, but soon follows is a gun to her back held by Gage.

The helicopter has just landed, pushing dust and wind in our direction. I nudge Barge, though he is already calling in to move in stealthy. All the sudden the cop cars flip their blinding lights on in the direction of the helicopter, and the helicopter is circled with officers ready to shoot. Amid the chaos, I hear "Holdings" being shouted. It only took me a few seconds to notice the voice is coming from the man I loathe. I stand up and begin to walk closer, with Barge and Nash at my back.

"Holdings. Good to officially meet you, man. Too bad it's over this slut." He laughs like an evil clown. I grit my teeth, waiting for the next punchline. Walking closer, I easily catch the fear washed over Amity's face so I give her a wink to reassure her she will be fine. "You need to let us leave and not follow. Or do you want her dead if you can't have her?" He tightens his grip on her arm, sliding the barrel of the gun down her cheek and neck, taunting her with her own death.

"As long as she's alive and happy, I don't care who she is with. That is what real love means. Giving the other all of you with no expectation in return. Not the sick shit you try to push on her."

"Don't provoke him, Blake," Barge whispers behind me. I flip him the finger, letting him know I am over this bullshit game.

"What do you want, Gage? We know it's not her. She is just an object to you."

"An object in my possession, might I remind you, Holdings. Maybe I just need to put us both out of miseries and kill her now. How does this worthless whore have two men who can have any pussy in the world but drooling for hers."

I hear the click of the safety and shout, "NO," rushing toward her, only to be toppled to the ground with Nash on top of me. Guns fire in every direction. I look up to see blood splattered all over Amity's body, eyes wide as she goes down with Gage. Nash is still pressing me down in the ground until everyone ceases fire. I finally get my arm unlocked from his hold and elbow him in the nose. With his release, I rush to Amity's side, pulling her body to mine. Blood is everywhere, death fills the air as I rock her back and forth, screaming and cursing God for all he is worth. Tears blur my eyes until I can no longer see.

CHAPTER 17:
BLAKE

I keep going over in my head how the hell we even got here. Clint even came home from Brazil for the "family emergency" as my mother called it. Granted his level head has been needed to handle the damn media circus. Everyone's on edge wondering what I am going to do next. I honestly don't know what the fuck else I can do. The bastard is dead. I've thrown and broken all my dining chairs. Punched a hole through my wall. Threatened everyone I love to leave me the hell alone. Cussed out a handful of staff then had to bring donuts the next day to apologize. Now I am all alone in the chapel crying and begging for life and forgiveness. At this point, I should be thankful she is alive, but I need her to wake up. I need her to *be her* in all her essence. I need her to cuss me out, tell me I'm being a mutant or diva, then tell me she loves me.

It's been six days in a drug induced coma. Tomorrow her doctor wants to start pulling her out of the coma. He said the swelling has gone down tremendously, and her vitals are looking great.

How anyone escaped that night unscathed besides Gage and Amity is unbeknownst to me. His blood from the shot to the head was splattered all over Amity. When he fell, he took her down with her, and by a miracle, only her shoulder landed on the gun, setting it off. It was a clean shot all the way through, not severing any major vessels. The worst was her head slamming against a rock, knocking her unconscious with instant swelling and bleeding. I can't be thankful enough for the paramedics who were already at the scene ready to handle all outcomes. Though they did have to pry her from my arms, especially once they noted she was alive. Her pulse was faint, but one was there.

For six long painstaking days, I have been waiting. Sitting in this chapel when the nurses come in to clean her and change her bandages. Wondering if this is some penance I'm being given on the life I've led. Sure I whored around, but never hurt anyone. I've led a wholesome, honest career supported by family traditions. And when I say honest, I mean mostly because I am not above blackmailing some bastard to get my way. Sure I am pampered, a mother's boy, and have high expectations, but I've also earned my place here. I help those in need, volunteer when I can, well since I met Amity, and strive to attend church at least one Sunday a month.

Surprisingly that crass girl I love so damn much has changed me for the better.

Two days have passed since they stopped the coma meds. We are now like floating ducks, paddling beneath the surface with anticipation. We have been able to catch several twitches and grasps of her hands since yesterday. I swear she even squeezed my hand last night when I laid my head on her bed to sleep. I'm ready for her to wake up so I can crawl in this bed and hold her close. Right now, her body has seemed so stiff, I would hate to hurt her because she's unable to vocalize.

I've only been home twice just to shower and meet with my cleaning lady so she can get my apartment back in order for when I bring Amity home. We will be selling her apartment immediately once she is released. Tilly and Lana have been keeping Hamlet, and we have a plan to sneak him up here once Amity wakes up. I know she is going to want all of those big goofballs' snuggles and kisses. I've even had Nash help me look at some properties out by him and Willa so we can move out of this apartment life. Have some property of our own to grow. I can always carpool to the office with Nash on days our schedules align. I also know Amity would love to be closer to the ranch. The only thing I am unsure of is her job at the college. I'm not sure what her expectations are or theirs. I know she loves teaching and is a huge asset to the program. My head has been swarming with ideas and what-ifs, I just need her to wake the hell up so we can make decisions.

The day has been wasted away with me sitting here, groveling to my girl to wake up, writing a travel list of all the places we are going to go, learning how to rope a cow via YouTube to impress her, which then put me on a thread of Amity's old rodeo competitions from college. I was even enlightened with the YouTube video of her riding an actual bull for eight seconds. No wonder the incident at the ranch gave her no distress, unlike me who thought she was going to be punctured with a horn and split in two. Then stomped all over untill she was part of the soil. This daredevil unapologetically shameless woman I find myself infatuated with is going to be the near death of me, but I would never want to change her unyielding fire for life. Out of the corner of my eye, I spot movement then followed by groaning. I jump up, fling open the door, shout for a nurse, then rush back to Amity's side.

"Hey, princess, I'm right here. Take it easy."

CHAPTER 18:
SWEET DREAMS

My eyes flutter open, adjusting to the bright fluorescent lights above me. I hear a voice pulling me out of the fog my mind and body are lost in. Excruciating pain rocks my body when I move, but I know I want to be where that voice is. Then I hear several others saying my name, with an even brighter light being shoved into my eyes. Causing my head to want to bust open. I'm able to get my arm up to block my eyes.

Hoaresely, "fucking pineapples, get that damn light away from me." I hear a deep chested laugh that pulls my attention to the left of me. Once my eyes fully adjust, I see him. I reach for his face. When my palm grapples the thicker than usual scruffiness of his face, I begin to cry. Blake's alive, I'm alive. The whole night flashes through my mind quickly, sending a deep shiver through me.

"Are you cold," I hear the nurse ask. I try to speak again, but my mouth is desert dry. Soon, a straw is inserted in my mouth and allowing the water to wash the dry grit away. Once finished, I look up at everyone. My parents, several nurses, a doctor, and my Blake all surround my bed.

"How are you feeling?" The doctor asks.

"Like I just took part in a bull run and lost." They laugh, but seriously, my head hurts like hell.

"Well now that you are awake and communicating, we can manage your pain medications more thoroughly. You have been asleep for many days, but we are all very excited to see you awake and present. I will order a CT to be completed by this evening to monitor and compare it with your last results. Please let the nurse know if you need anything, and I'll be back around in the morning."

"Thank you," I say. Followed by all the thanks you for those around me. The nurse continues to take my vitals again while another injects more drugs into my IV. My parents shower me in hugs, and we chat about what has been going on the last several days. Blake has stepped out in the hallway to call Nash so he can let the girls know I'm awake.

"He barely left your side, sweetie. We have all been worried sick, but we have all been extra worried about Blake. He has not been handling this situation well at all." I look at my mama in amusement, thinking when has Blake Holdings ever handled anything well outside of his control? Deddy lets me know he has been helping out with Nevada over at the ranch so he was not neglected. That life seems to have pulled everyone in a million different directions since that horrifying night. Soon they say their good-byes, and Blake struts in causally with his arms crossed. He stops at the foot of my bed.

"Amity, I'm going to say what I need to say. You are not going to interrupt me, throw anything at me or argue with me when I'm done. You understand?"

I raise my eyebrow in confusion.

"I need you to say you understand me, Amity."

I'm immediately taken back with the sternness in his voice and figure I better play along. "I understand, Blake."

He takes a deep breath before unraveling before me. "I swear to Heaven and Hell, Amity, you pull some dimwitted stunt like that ever again, I will tie you up myself and leave you in a cage. What the hell were you thinking? Don't fucking answer that! I know what you were thinking, because I found your love letter to me. You think you are so smart and brave, but guess what, princess? I'm smarter and braver. You will never risk your life for me again. Understood?"

I'm still in shock over being reamed like an intolerant schoolgirl, but I nod my head yes.

"You don't get to make life decisions without my two cents. One, if you thought I would let you just disappear without searching for you, you needed your damn head examined before all this bullshit. Second, if you thought I would handle your estate within a year of you not returning, another big NO. That would have meant I had given up. I will never give up on you or us. You, Amity Jean Mercer, are mine. When the time comes for your last breath, it will be mine also." He pauses and stalks to the right side of my bed, hovering over me. "When you are released, you will be moving in with me. Your stuff is being moved as we speak, and you will place your apartment up for sale within the next two months. Then we have a wedding in a few weeks that will be carrying on as initially planned. From there, you will help me pick out a house with some land that we will move into as a family. In the midst of house hunting, we will be going on a month long honeymoon to Belize then over to the Islands of Antigua and St. Lucia. Once you spring free from here, you need to make a decision about your teaching job. I know you love your job, but I won't lie if putting a baby in you and conjoining you to me forever doesn't get my dick hard."

My thoughts are swirling until he gives me that charming smolder that melts my heart. He leans down, placing a kiss on my forehead. All I can say is I agree to every last detail. Honestly, it could be all the meds I feel taking effect that has my giddy and agreeable, but I have time to deal with some of this stuff once I'm feelin' well enough to think. My heavy eyelids close as thoughts of settlin' down and babies with Blake fill my dreams.

Four days later, I am finally being released home. I just hope today goes better than yesterday. Blake has been stuck to me like glue for the last sixty plus hours, and I need space. I threw the water pitcher at his head yesterday to reiterate I meant business. This was all after I had awakened with a headache and him asking if I was okay for the millionth time in a twenty-minute span.

"No, I am not fine. At what point did you think I was actually fine? When the flowers were being sent? Or when a gun was held to my head? Oh, let me guess, when I was laying in this fucking bed in a coma!" I had shouted at him right before the water pitcher went soaring into his head.

He called me a crazy bitch, I just shrugged my shoulders, then he stormed out of the room. He was back in two hours with a box of my favorite donuts, and we moved on. I was in a piss-poor mood. Like everything over the last month just toppled over me. Leaving me gasping for air in a hole I kept sinking in. I'm also not used to being waited on hand and foot, yet Blake is so doting, it's making my skin crawl. I'm ready to be out of here, accomplishing life on my own two feet again. I've already talked to my director and decided I will head back to work in February. That gives me time to rest, get married, and go on this crazy long honeymoon with Blake. If and when, I do become pregnant, I'll continue to work, and then we can plan for the future then.

BLAKE

My girl is finally home in our apartment after what has been a month from the center of hell. Once again, Amity has persevered, but her loss of independence over this time is keen to the emotional rollercoaster she has taken. We've had our petty ass fights because I feel I need to care for her, she feels she has everything handled. Perspectively, she honestly does. I just need her thick skull to realize I'm not the enemy but the person who obsessively loves her and wants her to want for nothing. Again, neither of us are great at relationships. I keep that tidbit of information that I am her second, she is my first in my head. We honestly have no clue how to relationship. We only know how to do us, and I am completely content with that knowledge. This woman has turned my world upside down, my whole being belongs to only her. Now to remove all breakable objects she could potentially throw while she is sleeping.

CHAPTER 19:
VEGAS?

In less than eighteen hours, I am going to be Mrs. Amity Jean Mercer-Holdings. *Shit, pineapples!* I'll be Casanova Blake Holdings' wife. What a whirlwind this year has been. Let alone, if you asked me even eight months ago, marriage was never in the cards for me, and then even three months ago, I believed my newly founded fairytale would be destroyed. Now here we are at my parents' house for rehearsal dinner. The pastor is running late for actual rehearsal, so I take the time to rummage through my thoughts. The irony of the two of us together is not lost on me. I've heard the rumors of bets of who will be the first to cheat or Blake will leave me within a year due to boredom. Many don't know my past, but it seems a plethora of people are well inapt in Blake's. I have had the sheer pleasure of watching women throw themselves at him, only to be ignored. Not even a glance. Even men have propositioned to share me in bed to get a piece of him. Still not sure how I feel about any of it, other than I hundred percent trust Blake. Sometimes I feel as if his eyes are trained to only see me in a crowded room. No matter where I'm at, he finds me. He can be in mid conversation, but I know by just a look in his eyes and smirk, I have his full attention.

Last night at Paramour was no different. We decided to partake in a joint one last night of freedom bachelorette/bachelor party. I was skeptical at first about being back there, but everyone wanted to make sure I only keep the best memories from a place I enjoy so much. They were right of course. The night was filled with dancing with my girls, drinking, singing, and grinding up against my Adonis of a man. His confidence still uncanny, and fuck, if it's not the most attractive personality trait he owns. It just flows off him with ease, making the devil himself shake on his throne. Especially when his arms are wrapped around me. He becomes untouchable to everyone else. A scene from last night grabs my full attention from the rehearsal gathering.

When the night ended, he offered me the chance to bring home anyone I wanted to join in his plans for me. Without a thought, I turned to him and whispered, "You are all I need tonight, Blake, and every day and night after." Then pulled him by his tie to a dimly lit room on the roof, shoved him into a chair, revealed I had no panties before I crawled down his body, unzipping his pants along my way. Once his cock was free, my tongue licked and teased him. Finding more pleasure in that only I can un-do this man to his core. He growled obscenities and moaned in pleasure, fisting his hand in my hair to take him deeper. *Don't mind if I do*, I thought.

At one point, he was curved down my throat as I sucked. Couldn't care less, my eyes were watering, and my gag reflex was holding tight. The look of his hooded eyes rolling in the back of his head when I gently bit down, pulling my teeth in an upward motion, before sliding them back down was worth every ounce of pain. He was so unraveled by the time he came. His hands strongly squeezed both sides of the armrest of the chair that I could see his veins on the back of his hands popping. Blake was shaking by the time I licked his last drop. I tried to stand up, but he pounced, pushing my back to the floor.

"What was that, Amity?" he breathlessly growled out.

I gave him a wink. "Just reminding you where you belong."

"Oh, princess, I know exactly where I belong. Would you like me to show you?" he asked tauntingly.

Only to encourage him more, I nibbled my bottom lip. "You might need to before I get lost in that crowd over there." He looked over and behind me where the door opened to the dance floor. Clearly anyone that walked by had been having a nice show. Blake's look was dangerous and full of lust when his baby blues met mine. I could see the fire burning behind them, never wavering, as he slid himself into my folds. My hand moved to touch his chest, but he quickly pinned my arms above my head.

"You are going to take me without touching," he gritted out. His other arm slipped under my back, arching my back, as he sucked and bit my nipples through my dress. I squirmed underneath him with the need to feel every part of him on me. Once he released my wrists, to pull down my dress to access my naked breasts, I took the opportunity to rough his hair up and pull myself up to bite his neck. A beastly growl escaped him, then he flipped us to where I was straddling him as he held my body close to his in an upright position. It only took a few seconds once the hair raises on my arm that I notice we have eyes on us. Blake is practically still dressed where I have my dress wrapped around my waist. Not that I ever cared for an audience other than my family. Blake sensed the onlookers. "Show them who you belong to, Princess."

I lean back, groping my own breasts as he nips over them. "Blake," I shriek, as I can feel his palms tighten around my waist.

In his rough, hoarse voice, he groaned out, "Own me, Amity." With that, I threw my body against his as I rode him into pure blissfulness. My core clenched his shaft while I slowly wound down the movements of my hips.

A kick to the ankle under the table brings me back to the present. "Girl, where did you go?" I lightly laugh, looking at Tilly.

"Don't worry I captured her lost in a sexual bliss state of mind."

My head whips to face Lana. "You wouldn't?"

"She would," a laughing Willa waltzes by grabbing Lana's camera before I can steal it from her. The girls are laughing their asses off, but when I look up, I'm locked on baby blues. He winks, as if he knew exactly where my mind was. He waves his phone in the air, gesturing for me to look at mine as he stands with his brothers. I look down.

Asshat: "Wild guess… Were you thinking of last night?"
Me: Maybe. (winking face emoji)
Asshat: I bet you are soaked.
Me: You comin' over here to do somethin' bout it?
Asshat: You change my name on your phone yet?

I let out a loud laugh because hell no I haven't. He pissed me off yesterday morning over a damn rug, so I've refused to change it.

Asshat: I'll take that as a NO.
Me: I'm thinking about it.
Asshat: Well, take your time, princess. I'll just be over thinking about eating you out and licking you all over.

I look back up at him, his grin spread wide across his face.
Asshat: Don't threaten me with those ice daggers. You know how they get me harder for you.

I stern my face more, but before I can rush over there to tease him more, I'm pulled into another room with my friends. "What are ya'll up to?"

"Nothing. Pastor is about five minutes out, so we are about to start rehearsal," Lana states.

"I don't even know why we need a rehearsal."

"Just part of the process, Am. Indulge us."

"Just so you know, this whole wedding is to indulge everyone. I'm still counting on a Vegas wedding."

Willa comes over to hug me. "Oh, my spitfire, Amity. You will thank us all one day. Now, everything has been taken care of, you just have to get dressed tomorrow, smile, and walk down the aisle to Blake. Just try to take in the smaller moments, because it truly does happen in a blink of an eye."

"I promise," I sniffle as the four of us form a group hug.

"You ready to gift Blake your wedding present tonight?"

"I think so, if the band is ready." I already feel my hands gettin' clammy which singing on stage never makes me nervous like this. I guess because this means somethin'. Givin' him another piece of me.

We survived, or I should say, I survived rehearsal. Blake asked a million and one questions about positioning. Made last minute changes to the marrying of the candles ceremony along with saying traditional vows on top of the vows he requested we write ourselves. I had to keep reminding him the wedding is at the Crenshaw Ranch and that things will look slightly different. Lana finally had to calm Groom-Zilla down before he had a bridal meltdown. It took all my power to keep my laughs to slight giggles in the midst of the chaos.

Pastor Bryan even looked over at me halfway through and asked if I still wanted to proceed with marrying Blake tomorrow. I thought Blake was going to banish him that instant until Nash stepped in with a glass of scotch to take Blake's edge off. I promised the Pastor that Blake will be better behaved tomorrow and calmer. After what should have taken thirty minutes turned into two hours plus more picture taking, we finally were able to sit and eat. Blake and I had our own special table that looked out to everyone so we could still mingle. I didn't want them cooking all day either, so they catered in one of my favorite Mexican restaurants, also family to Willa and Nash, Panchito's. Flaming steak and chicken fajitas with delicious Texas-style nachos with all the toppings and guacamole for everything. I starved all day, just so I could pig out tonight and not feel guilty if my dress was a little snug tomorrow.

BLAKE

I'm thankful to finally sit down next to Amity and breathe. She leans over and whispers, "We can still make it to Vegas?"

"Tempting, but no, princess," I state with a smile. She shrugs her shoulders then goes back to chowing down on her overly large stuffed tortilla with no care in the world of being ladylike. Which only makes me love her more. I'm eight scotches in now, and Clint and Nash have given me the lecture to chill and enjoy myself.

With everything that has gone on over the last few months, I just want this wedding to be perfect. Selfish me, I know I planned this wedding to my standards as Amity wanted no part in planning. Hell, even if she did, she would have been vetoed out I'm sure with my ideas. Lana is a saint dealing with me, and for that, she will be getting a nice-sized check from me as a gift. She wanted to do this as a wedding gift for Amity, but she poured her heart and time into making all the visions come true. I watch Amity take a sip of wine, with her hair tied up off her neck, dawning a blue laced dress that hugged her body. She looks the epitome of grace in this moment, and I quickly snap a picture with my phone. Once she hears the camera, her face turns to me. "Hey, there, man. No candid shots."

"Man?" I question her.

She laughs, "You caught me off guard." She smiles widely, and I lean in kissing her cheek. She pops a chip smothered in guac into her mouth, and I just watch her. Snapping more candid pictures of the faces she makes when her mouth is stuffed.

"You look like a chipmunk trying to hoard all the chips."

She giggles. "I can't help it. It's so fuckin' delicious." Then she's diving in for another. Leaving her to it, I go about filling my tortilla with all the fixins as the Golden Girls have taught me to say. Halfway through eating, our parents stand up to give speeches. Both heartfelt and tearful. My parents never thought I would settle down, and Amity's parents thought she would never love again.

Once the sopapillas are served with three different dipping sauces of chocolate, caramel, and raspberry, Lana comes over to grab Amity. "I promise to have her right back." They both shoot me an 'up to no good' smile. When I turn around, I spot all four of the Golden Girls disappearing around the corner. Clint comes down to sit next to me as if he might have an inkling of what is going on. But nonetheless, he doesn't say a word about the wedding, just discusses the upcoming rodeo in February, and talks of the house he just purchased in Brazil. We all decided to have a permanent stake down there and grow Holdings Oil. With Clint being the only one not tied down, he offered to take over the South America Branch with Nash and I traveling to him when needed. It makes sense for him to purchase a house and be comfortable during the transition and moving forward. I've noted twenty minutes have gone by and still no Amity or the rest of them.

Then the outside lights dim and outsteps Amity on the planked dance floor in a lavish red sequined ball gown. The band starts to play, and the lights brighten up a bit to get a read on people's faces. People's faces who all seem to be staring at me waiting for a reaction. I'm already stunned to see Amity looking gorgeous and sultry with the split up to her hip, but then she opens her mouth to sing, and I am floored. She sings at gatherings, around the apartment, jams out in the car, but she has never once sung a song to me.

"Wisemen say, only fools rush in… But I can't help falling in love with you. Shall I stay? Would it be a sin? If I can't help falling in love with you." She starts off sweet and soft, then powers her voice up with the next chorus. I'm blown away and feel as if a volcano of emotions has erupted within. Amity continues to sing, strutting over in her heels to me. She sits in my lap, singing directly to me, freezing me in place. She belts out the last couple of lines, then plants a breathtaking kiss on my lips.

Speaking back into the microphone, she says, "I love you, Blake Lane Holdings. I look forward to walking toward you and our future tomorrow." I lean in kissing her temple, then she stands, taking my hand to stand up next to her. "Y'all know me enough to know I hate crying, but it seems all I have been able to do these last several months. This man next to me makes me soft, so I need to toughen him up more I guess." The crowds hollers and laughs. "On a serious note, I just want to thank everyone here tonight. Whether you have raised me by birth, became my new deddy through marriage, or became my family through the best girls I could have in my life, thank you for being there through all the bad shit and good. For molding me into the person I am today. To my girls, or as Blake refers to us, the Golden Girls, y'all are my anchor in the rough seas, the wind calling me home, and the feathers that guide me. To the family I am marrying into, thank you for creating a son who has a heart like mine. I love you all so much and not once did you ever hesitate to welcome me with open arms. But I can't promise I won't accidentally break anything else either."

All laugh, and Amity gets the overwhelmed giggles. Then she takes a deep breath and continues, "To the man I am marrying tomorrow, I am saving most of my thoughts for these damn vows you made me write." I kiss her neck then give her my smolder, knowing she will forgive me. "Y'all see the face I can't say no to, right? Anyhow, I do want to tell you before the night ends and we go our separate ways, I love you. I hope you enjoyed your wedding gift as I was not sure what else to gift the man who has everything, but then I realized I had already given you my heart, but now you have my soul." Her glacier eyes stare deep into mine with longing.

I quickly pull her into me and dip her down into a kiss where our tongues entwine like vines, never wanting to part.

"Save it for tomorrow," my father shouts.

"Don't make me grab the hose," Nash yells next.

I pull away from her. "I love you so fucking much." Then pulling her back up to stand next to me, I grab her mic. "Huge thank you to the Mercers for hosting this stellar evening and for your incredible daughter. Like Amity, I will save my words for tomorrow, but please note from the bottom of my heart and families, we love her to pieces. Now, alright everyone, Good Night. I need everyone bright-eyed, and bushy-tailed for this wedding tomorrow. Then we can party into the night." I drop the mic into Lana's hands and kiss my soon-to-be bride one more time. The girls tug her one way as the guys push me out the other door. They even confiscated our phones until after the wedding tomorrow.

We head back out into the city to stay at my apartment for the night, while the girls head to the Crenshaw Ranch.

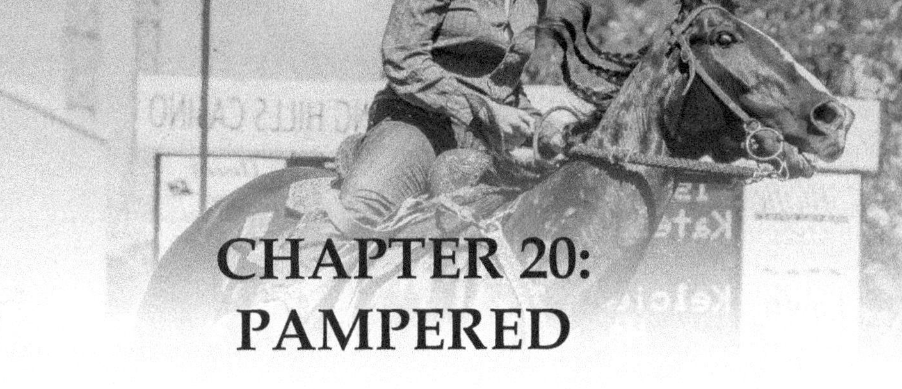

CHAPTER 20: PAMPERED

Nash must have heard we partied hard until the early morning hours, as he sent his "butler" Grant with the magical elixir so we could be functioning humans today. I can't even say we partied. We just stayed up playing card games, taking shots, and then taunting me with calling Blake. Needless to say, the bags under my eyes look like trenches. I toss myself back into the bed and hide under the covers. Hamlet jumps in the bed, using his snout to find me, giving away my hiding spot.

All three girls proceed to drag me out of the bed. "Come on, Amity. It's already eleven, and the moms just pulled in with an entourage of hair and makeup artists."

"Ugh, just come get me with thirty minutes to spare, and I can get myself ready."

"I swear I have never seen a bride more inclined to pass on her own wedding day. Maybe we should call Nash for reinforcements." I hear Tilly loudly whisper to Willa.

Pulling the covers off my head but wrapping them around me, I glare at them both. "What reinforcements?"

Lana strolls in. "Oh, I don't know. Maybe letting the media head over here. Or decking Nevada out diamonds for when you ride him over. Or allow kids into the ceremony?"

"FIIINNNE, I'm up! What do I need to do?"

"Firstly, go take a shower. The wax lady will be here in an hour to spruce you up, then you can get your hair done. Grab a small snack. Oh, and drink lots of water today. Then it will be time for makeup, dress, pictures, wedding, then more pictures, then the reception. So, chop chop!"

Looking at Tilly and Willa, I mock-whisper, "When the hell did Lana get so bossy?"

"I guess since she planned a wedding in four months with Blake," Tilly says, laughing.

"No, I get it. He either makes you grow a backbone or want to crawl in a deep hole to rot."

We laugh, then Lana pokes her head back in. "NOW, Amity. You have ten minutes." I slowly walk into the bathroom, where she had already started the shower. The bathroom is steamed up. As I step in, I let the hot water cinch my skin and roll over my body. Probably the most relaxed moment I will have all day.

I was right. The shower was the only miniscule amount of relaxation I have had all day. I barely was able to grab a granola bar before I was thrown to the wax lady, who left me with a mere landing strip as far as hair goes on my bikini area. Then tossed over to get a manicure and pedicure all while answering questions about I don't even know what between my mama and Mrs. Holdings. They were like two squirrels running around a tree with topics of conversation. Then I was placed in the hands of the hairstylist who tugged and curled my hair. Lana had decided on a loose curl, twist updo at the nape of my neck with small braids from the front, twisting in the back. Accentuated with a platinum vintage diamond leaf comb that slides in at the top. Once done, my makeup was finally applied. I honestly can't think of a day in my life where I wore so much makeup, but I get it. This needs to last all day for pictures, the wedding, more pictures, make out sessions I plan on having with my husband, and the reception.

"Alright, Am, time to put your dress on." Lana comes in already looking gorgeous in her stunning cornflower chiffon one-shoulder dress, with her wavy blonde hair half pulled up with a mini matching hair comb to mine in the back. Followed by Tilly in the same dress, with her hair in an updo with loose curls framing her face. Then Willa in a longer version of the same dress with her hair done up in a messy modern ponytail with a fishtail braid alongside. A slight laugh slips through my lips, as their makeup all matches for the most part, same dress, but their hair all represents their style, and I love it.

Willa has the dress in her hands. "Are you ready for the big reveal?"

"I still can't believe you didn't pick out your own wedding dress. Let alone, have not tried it on," Tilly pipes in.

"Y'all, know I did not want a huge wedding. Besides, I have complete confidence in Lana and Blake to pick out the perfect dress for me."

Willa loses it. "Blake has seen your dress? I thought it was just Lana." I look at Lana.

"Calm down, snapples, Y'all are all wound up today. First off, I have been measuring Amity every week even up to two days ago to ensure her dress will fit perfectly. Second of all, I had Blake pick out his top five favorites, and then from there, I chose one so he would still be surprised. And might I add, he made it tough. Every dress he could have picked out for Amity would have looked stunning on her and fit her style. This one kept catching my eye and screamed Amity to me above the rest. It's a vintage, elegant high neck with lace, with a complete open back. The cut will hug your body, and the lace is see-through on the top, like on the arms."

"Well hell, now I'm excited. Let's get this puppy on me." It takes all four of us to wrangle me in this dress, but once on, it's stunning, and we all start to tear up. All topped off with my brand-new distressed leather Shyanne Sienna Metalico boots with floral embroidery.

"Don't ruin your make-up, Am."

"Look who's talking, Wil." We laugh and know there is no use in trying to stop the tears. So much emotion is behind these tears. Trauma, abuse, heartbreak, struggle, love, happiness, self-perseverance, and acceptance. These girls have lived every moment of all of it with me.

"I'm so happy for you, Am. My heart is bursting with joy for you after everything that occurred. You're alive and here. And now get to marry that man that truly was created for you," Lana speaks.

I tug her in my arms for a tight hug. "I know this could have not been easy for you to plan, so know it means the world to me that you took this on. And I promise you, one day soon, you will find your match. The one that worships you like the goddess you are because you deserve nothing less." She smiles through her tears, and then we all find ourselves in a group hug again.

"Flippin' snapples. Now we all need touch-ups. Let me go grab a few of the makeup people. I'll be right back."

"Oh, honey bunches, you look so pretty. Blake is going to faint."

"Thank you, Mama." I lean over to kiss her on the cheek. "No tears, Mama. Lana will have all our asses."

She slightly slaps my arm. "Oh, Amity. Watch your language today. It's a beautiful day." I give her my, *I'll give it my best try*, grin.

I feel like I have had a camera in my face ever since I woke up this morning with all the candid shots and then those of me getting ready, plus a few solo shots in the dress. Then we spent an hour doing group pictures, and I have to say the men look on fire in their deep navy-blue suits with cornflower blue ties to match the bridesmaids. If that is any indication of how my man will look at the end of the aisle, I know I'm in trouble. We take several typical wedding group shots with just the girls, then the guys, and all together, but then several fun ones also. Like the guys holding me up in their arms, a few where it looks as if I'm running away and they capture me, and one where we climbed my favorite tree, very carefully. Several in front of the barn doors and by the fences with the cows in the background.

When I thought I was getting a breather when my ladies and the guys were sent to do photos with Blake over at the main house, my photographer stayed to get some solo shots of me and then deddy brought out Nevada for the photoshoot. He sure looks mighty handsome all groomed with a brand-new black leather double bridle adorned with Swarovski crystals across the browband. Cornflower blue ribbon weaved into his black mane. Deddy and the photographer help me get on the back of Nevada. We decided bareback would be the best way to go today to not have to deal with the saddle with me in a dress. Plus, it's near seventy degrees today, regardless that we are in the month of December. We take several of me laying across him with my train hanging down along his side, then a few with me sitting up. I think one my favorites will be the close up of my face with his on the side of his blue eye that matches mine. His other eye is brown, and I love how his mix-matched eyes play into his personality. I can tell he is feeling himself today with all the hustle going on at the ranch, me dressed up, and the photographer all over him.

Kissing his muzzle, then running my hands along the side of it, I murmur, "You are such a good boy. You ready to do this today?" He places his nose into my neck. "I'll take that as a yes."

"Hey, Amity." I turn to see Lana. "We have about an hour left before the ceremony starts, but we thought we could do a cute photo session with you and Blake, but y'all cannot look at each other. He is currently blindfolded, and I need to put one on you also, until we can get you positioned."

"Um, okay." She places the blindfold carefully over my eyes and face, then she takes my hand and guides me to the other side of Nevada.

Then I hear Clint's voice. "Bro, trust me. I'm not going to trip you."

I giggle knowing Blake must be a nervous wreck not being in control at this moment. "Princess, is that you?"

"It is, all mighty one."

"Such a smartass already today."

"Well, I've been awake since the break of dawn, so shall be expected." He laughs, and my heart clenches because I feel like it has been forever since I've seen him.

"Alright you two, Nevada is between the two of you. There is to be no peeking. Once we back you up to be against Nevada, I will place your hands together, and Clint and I will remove the blindfolds. Again, we are taking these quickly, and no peeking. Capeesh?"

We both answer, "Capeesh."

Once our fingers lace together under Nevada's neck, my breath hitches. I know he can feel the heat and sparks flowing between us. He squeezes my hand diligently. I'm so tempted to move and look at him, but Lana is giving me the evil eye already. I hear Clint threatening Blake not to move. "Just look towards me now," the photographer asks. Within five minutes, she is done, and I am blindfolded again. Blake squeezes my hand tightly one more time before we are separated.

"See you soon," he shouts back to me.

Finally, I am whisked back to Willa's old cabin for some water and touch ups. Willa and Tilly show up with smiles and giddiness, letting me know how gorgeous my soon to be husband looks today. My eyes pop out of my head, when Tilly hands me a Tiffany box. Their blue is so distinctive along with the ribbon. "This is from Blake."

"I told him I did not want a gift because we are going on a month-long honeymoon."

"You know that boy doesn't listen to a thing anyone tells him," Willa adds. I shake my head in agreement as I undo the ribbon, slipping the top off.

"O my fuckin' pineapples." I pull out a platinum chain necklace with a diamond studded horseshoe with matching earrings. "He has lost his damn marbles." They laugh, and Willa takes the necklace from my hand to put on me. I fumble with removing the earrings I was wearing to replace them with the diamond horseshoes.

Time seemed to move slowly until Lana announced it was time. We drove the gator slowly back down to the barn where I mounted Nevada, then the girls and my mom headed down to the where the ceremony is being held. I was told all I have to do is ride Nevada down the driveway, take a left by the large oak then a right after the fence. I got this. "We got this. Right boy?" I ask, petting Nevada on the neck to hopefully calm my jittery nerves down. I ride him to the aisle to meet deddy. I focus on him to refrain from looking at Blake. Knowing that if I do, I may fall off this horse. Once down, dress adjusted, I turn to link my arm with my deddy's. It's then I look up, and my breath is taken away.

CHAPTER 21:
THE GROOMS DAY

I woke up this morning ready to find Amity, steal her, and rush off to Vegas. My brothers and Josh did not let me out of their sight in fear of what I might do. We made it to the ranch at noon to start getting ready, and I was forbidden by Lana to walk the property to even take a peek at the setup. She wanted me to be surprised and just relax. Probably like Amity, I have had a photographer following me around since we arrived here. Lots of candid's of the guys and I taking shots and filling up our bourbon glasses. Anything to shake the nerves. Nash told me it was normal. Maybe the feeling is, but I am just ready to have her in my arms as my wife. The photo shoots earlier were fun and hilarious.

The golden girls told me I will have a heart attack once I see Amity. I believe them too. She is gorgeous naked, dressed down, glammed up, or in a damn trash bag. I've already tried to talk my pied piper down from getting hard during the ceremony in front of all the guests. Then when I was able to feel her near and hold her hand, I damn nearly lost my mind. To have her so close but not be able to caress her skin, kiss her soft luscious lips or capture her smile. Clint was threatening me through the whole shoot not to move a muscle or he would take me down. I decided not to anger him or destroy my suit, let alone ruin Amity's and I first look at the altar.

Walking out to the area where the ceremony is taking place, I am enamored with the site. A mixture of white flowers and wildflowers align the aisle with silver carpet. There are dim lights hanging in the air above the seats, floating from one tree to the next. The altar is four steps high, made from beautiful dark wood that blends in with the scenery. White flowers flow over the archway with touches of blues to match the wedding party. Lana really made my visions come to tuition, and they are more extraordinary than I had dreamed.

Cocktail hour started thirty minutes ago to keep the guests entertained prior to the ceremony. I make my rounds to greet guests with my brothers and Hamlet, with his matching bowtie, and tell my mother to stop crying for the hundredth time today or she will have a migraine before the ceremony even begins. She just swats at me and tells me to leave her alone. That she is allowed to cry all she wants because her baby boy is getting married. Father and I just roll our eyes and laugh. Before I know it, it's game time. Nash comes up and slaps me on the shoulder, "You ready for this?"

"Yes," is all I can muster out as we walk down the aisle to take our places. Hamlet is sitting between Nash and I, as we gave him the title of best man earlier this morning. Once all the guests are seated and Pastor Bryan steps up on to the altar after shaking our hands, the music begins to play.

"Whew," I let out a breath, stretching my arms out, cracking my neck in anticipation. The three golden girls walk down the aisle with their bouquets in hand, looking lovely. I already warned Nash to save the sexy eyes and smolder for Willa post ceremony. It was hard enough keeping their hands off each other during pictures. I hear Nevada's snort followed by a low whine. My girl is almost here. I look down at my hands, popping my fingers and taking in another deep breath. *Shit, this is happening.* The music changes, and I look up to find the breathtakingly dark angel I've known Amity to be dressed in white, looking as pure as Heaven itself. Stan helps her slide off Nevada and helps her straighten her dress, then hands her bridal bouquet of whites and blues to match the archway, where a few vines hang down almost to the ground.

Look at me. Come on, look at me, baby.

Amity finally locks eyes on me, causing my heart to halt. She keeps them locked on me as she strolls down the aisle, inching closer. I'm rocking on my heels by the time the two of them reach the altar, taking deep breaths. Pastor Bryan steps up. "Who gives Amity Jean Mercer away today in front of God, family and friends?"

"Me and her mama do," Stan states, leaning in, kissing Amity on her cheek, then shaking my hand before sitting down. Trembling, I take her hand in mine, helping her up the steps. Placing my hand on her bare lower back, I lean in to whisper in her ear, "You look ravishing, princess."

"Not too bad yourself, cowboy," she squeaks out with a wink. Pastor has us turn to each other and hold hands through his speech, and then the time comes for our vows. Amity is up first, and she looks like she could faint.

With a clearing of her throat, she begins, turning to the crowd. "Y'all, it's about to get deep up here, so bear with me." Making the guests laugh, and in Amity fashion, she has them in her palm. Turning back to me, her voice quivers as she continues. "Blake. My handsome Blake. There are a thousand things I need to say and a million I shouldn't say in front of people. Let's just see where we end up." She lets out a salacious laugh that has my body shaking with laughter. "I won't stand here in front of our loved ones and proclaim I choose you. I can't. Only because by some divine intervention, you were molded, sculpted, and pieced together for me. You once told me you believed the treacherous path I stumbled along led me to you. I believe that any path I walked down would have eventually led me to you. No other than you, has a heart like mine. That embodies my soul like you. That appreciates my sense of humor like you do. See. There is no choosing you, because there is no other option for me. Never has been. I'm looking forward to a lifetime of adventures with you, big or small. From timeouts underneath waterfalls, nights under the stars to lazy movie days, and Taco Tuesdays. I know every day will be an adventure with you by my side. So, I will stand here today, declare my love for you, my respect for you, my trust in you. I am yours. You have it all as I vow patience, honesty, and over-zealous adoring love for always and infinity."

My hand has been flexing at my side the whole time she spoke, now it's reached for her, pulling her to me. "I. fucking. Love. you," I say breathlessly, then smash my mouth on hers. My hands are planted on the sides of her face, and her arms are wrapped around my neck. The guests cheer.

Before I can go in for another kiss, we are being tugged away from each other, thanks to Lana and Clint. Pastor Bryan grins. "Blake, are you able to recite your vows now?"

Clearing my throat and opening my handwritten vows, I nod. "I am, sir." I take a second to stare into Amity's glacier blue eyes, to know I have her full attention. "Babe, Tinkerbell, peanut, honey badger, short stuff, and princess are just a few of the endearing nicknames I have tried on you during our time together. Granted you turned down all of those, though Princess stuck. Not because you elegantly hold yourself up to another standard or fragile, but because you are the total opposite. I could say you fight like a warrior, love like a hurricane, look like an angel, sing like a siren, ride like a cowboy. The truth is you are my warrior. Your love is wild. Full of calmness and raging winds, filled with torrential rain and sunshine. You are my dark angel that grounds me when needed, sheaths me with your wings in love and passion. Your voice draws me to you in a crowded room. You are the Queen of cowboys with your talent, crass mouth, and no rules for life. In all of this, you're mine.

"Now I can give you the greatest title I know, *my wife*. I vow to be the man you not only need but crave. I vow to be patient, honest and respect you. I vow to love you for always and infinity. Ending my vows with a quote from my favorite childhood author, A.A. Miline, 'If you live to be a hundred, I hope to live a hundred minus one day, so I never have to live without you.'"

Crocodile tears fall from her glaciers, but before I can move in, Clint's hand is on my shoulder, and Lana is stepping on Amity's dress train to hold her in place. Everyone applauds. I can hear sniffles and laughs amongst the show we must be putting on for them. "Now time for the rings," Pastor states. Hamlet pads over to me, and I pull the rings out of the ribbon that was tied to a small pillow on his back. I hand her mine, then take her hand. We manage to get through the I Do's quickly, rings placed on our fingers, then I am on her like Flash. Dipping her in my arms, sliding my tongue past her wet lips to dance with hers. Her hands are gripping my hair by the time I pull her back up with me and releasing her. With a chuckle, Pastor Bryan shouts, "I now introduce you to Mr. and Mrs. Holdings."

I throw her over my shoulder and hightail it down the aisle to get my wife alone for a few minutes. I hear Lana make the announcement, "Horderves and cocktails will be served on the west side of the barn as the bridal party does photos and last-minute touches are complete in the eatery."

'Where are we going?" Amity shouts from being upside down.

"Just over here behind the giant tree." Once there, I let her slide down my body, pushing her back into the tree. "I can't wait to get you out of this dress later. Fair warning, it may be ripped off you." My lips are determined to kiss every inch of her glowing face.

"You can't rip my wedding dress. I love it," she breathlessly says.

"I'll buy a new one," I groan, sucking her lower lip into my mouth.

"Blake and Amity Holdings, we need you at the altar now."

"Who the hell gave Lana a megaphone?"

"Good question," Amity retorts.

I move in for more making out, then, "Do not make us come search for you," stops me in my tracks.

"Fuck, now Clint. I guess we better show our faces."

She lets out her beautiful laugh. "Come on, husband, let's get this over with." Then she's dragging me back toward the altar.

CHAPTER 22:
PARTY

Lana and Blake out did themselves with the transformation of the ranch's eatery. Floor to ceiling vines of greenery and flowers. Long large clear pipes full of water immersed with petals floating inside. Tables covered in white and blue flower arrangements mixed in with horseshoes and cowboy hats. He somehow even hired my favorite BBQ restaurant all the way from Clute to cater. DJ's Bar-B-Que. I'm already eyeing out the best chopped brisket sandwich I have ever tasted drenched in spicy BBQ sauce and pickles. If only I could get over there, but Blake has me shaking hands with colleagues and distant relatives.

Does he not know I have barely eaten today?

Ten minutes later, I'm able to slip from his grip, mingle with a few of my own colleagues and friends, then grab a sandwich. "You could have just asked, and I would have had food brought to you?" his rough voice slips through my ear.

"You seemed busy," I retort, shrugging my shoulders, knowing he hates when I go all independent with my carefree attitude towards him. I hear a slight growl escape his lips.

"Never too busy to take care of you," he murmurs, kissing me on the temple, then stealing a bite on my sandwich.

"Bro, I need you to step away, before you get hurt. That was an illegal move." Blake laughs and tries to come in for another bite, only for me to shove the rest of the half sandwich in my mouth.

"I swear you are the classiest woman I know." I scrunch my nose and wink, due to my mouth full of brisket. "Keep making faces and see how many spankings you earn with my belt later." I finally swallow my food, stick my tongue out, and move quickly from his grasp to find my parents. Never looking back but knowing the Cheshire grin is spread wide across his face.

We finally get through all the toasts, the first dance, and dancing with our parents and friends, and finally, it's cake time. The wedding cake is five tiers alternating between chocolate and spice cake. It's lightly iced in a cream-colored buttercream to give it a semi-naked look, as Blake calls it. With a gold dusting to match the gold cursive H on the top tier. I love how it's rustic and classy. Then I see Blake pushing out a cart which I assume is his groom-cake, and I am bouncing on my heels in anticipation to see what he ends up doing. He unveils the first half, and I am speechless. No, it is not a dying armadillo cake but a huge cake version of Jetson the longhorn. Those of us there that day, and Willa's family are dying laughing. I shake my head at Blake, trying to catch my breath.

"What? You wouldn't let me send him to the slaughterhouse, so I figured cutting into a cake version was the next best thing." I place my hands on his face and pull him down to kiss softly on the lips.

"I love you Blake Holdings. Thank you for never a dull moment."

He winks. "Wait, I have one more surprise for you." Pulling back another cloth, I am welcomed with the site of a Shipley's donut tower. I gasp and jump into Blake's arms.

"I am totally eating these off your dick tonight and licking the icing off your body."

He drags his hand down his face. "Fuck me. We are having these damn things delivered every morning and night," he growls, leaning in for another kiss.

"Is it time to escape yet?"

"Almost. One more dance and drink with friends, and then we will disappear," he says before heading off to find Lana. When I peek down at my phone for the first time all night, I'm shocked that it's closing in on midnight. We also have a four a.m. flight to catch in the morning. Might as well keep on partying at this rate.

For a whole 'nother hour, we dance, drink, and sing until Lana sends everyone outside, and before we know it, Blake and I are runnin' through an aisle lined with our loved ones and sparklers. He stops at the end, dipping me for a kiss and holding me there, gazing into my eyes. His baby blues are full of lust.

Before jumping in the car, we say goodbye to our parents, thanking them again for everything, and Willa's parents for hosting this huge shindig. I give my girls the tightest hugs, knowing it will be a few weeks before I see them again, but I know we will chat every day. Blake does the same with his brothers. Deddy even kept Nevada out so I can hug him goodbye and tell him to behave while I'm gone. Hamlet is already in the car ready to go. We decided to bring him the big goof with us this time, since we missed him so much in Costa Rica. Once all loaded, we head straight to the airport to board the Holdings private jet.

And then we are off on our next adventure.

THE END

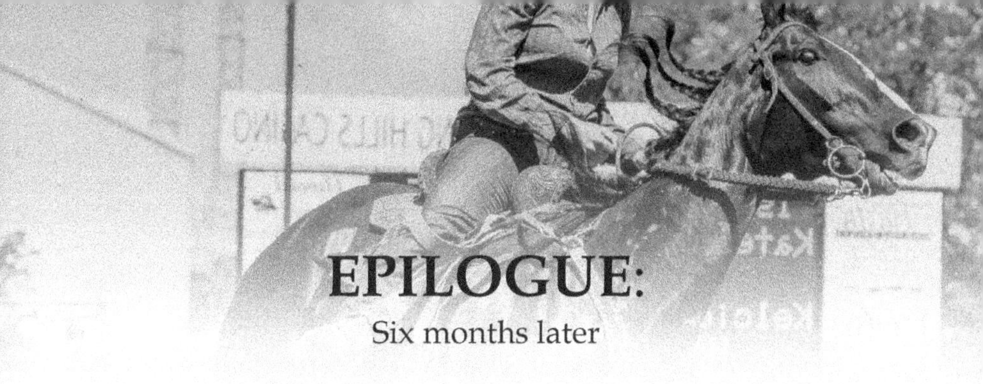

EPILOGUE:
Six months later

Life has been overwhelming to say the least, but I would not trade it for a minute. Once we arrived home from our honeymoon to bring in the New Year with our families and friends, Blake and I hit the ground running in January. My apartment sold, and then Blake and I purchased some land about two miles from my folks and five miles from Willa and Nash. I give my suggestions, I discuss colors, lighting and flooring with Blake when asked, but I basically handed the reins over to him once we picked out the house plans. The drive only adds an extra fifteen minutes for the both of us to work so we are excited to start this new adventure in several months once we can move in. Until then, we are living at Blake's place. I know Hamlet will be excited once we move out there to have space to run and roam. I'm still debating whether to move Nevada and get him a companion or leave him at the ranch.

Willa and I have been killing it at rodeos with our horses, and right now, our team is ranked number one in the state for ropin'. Nevada is holding third place in the state for reining, and we head to Tennessee in a month for another show. On top of that, I'm back to teaching at the college and still helping at the Crenshaw Ranch a few days a month. Luckily, their slow season falls during Willa and I's busiest season. She teaches also and has her own high school rodeo team she coaches on top of holding her own rodeo titles. I've been offered the chance to sing the

National Anthem at several events coming up this year so that is something new and exciting. And we try to make it over to Paramour at least one Thursday a month to unwind. I'm happy Blake is working back home with little travel right now, but Willa and I can tell the pressure of Clint not being on site and in Brazil puts on our men. But like always, they will persevere and be more of a force once they control the South America market in oil.

I eavesdropped in the barn last weekend when I heard Tilly and Dirks discussing something serious. I hid for a few minutes to try to figure out what was going on, but then Tilly rushed past me in tears. Still haven't been able to get her to spill the tea. She says she is fine, but she's definitely more on edge these days. Lana seems to be much happier since the wedding. Almost like she found her backbone again and is dabbling in wedding planning on the side of her full-time vet tech career.

Tonight, the girls and I, plus Nash and Blake, are meeting for dinner at Panchito's. Willa stated she had an announcement, and little do they know, Blake and I do too. Once we all arrived and settled with our bowls of guac and chips, chatting and catching up, Willa looks over to us from the end of the table and says, "Y'all! You won't believe who's pregnant?"

Everyone goes silent in anticipation. I turn to Blake with my accusing eyebrow raised, then look back to Willa. "Who told you?"

She looks at me confused. "Wait, what? I was announcing that Nash and I are having a baby." No one moves with the announcement.

"Hell fire," I say, laughing.

"Holy hades, shit a brick now, Amity, you too?" I nod, and then everyone screams with excitement over the two of us. Then Lana stands up and announces she is taking a solo trip to South America for the next year for work.

"What?" we all say in unison, leaving us all in shock.

Stay tuned for Lana's Story...

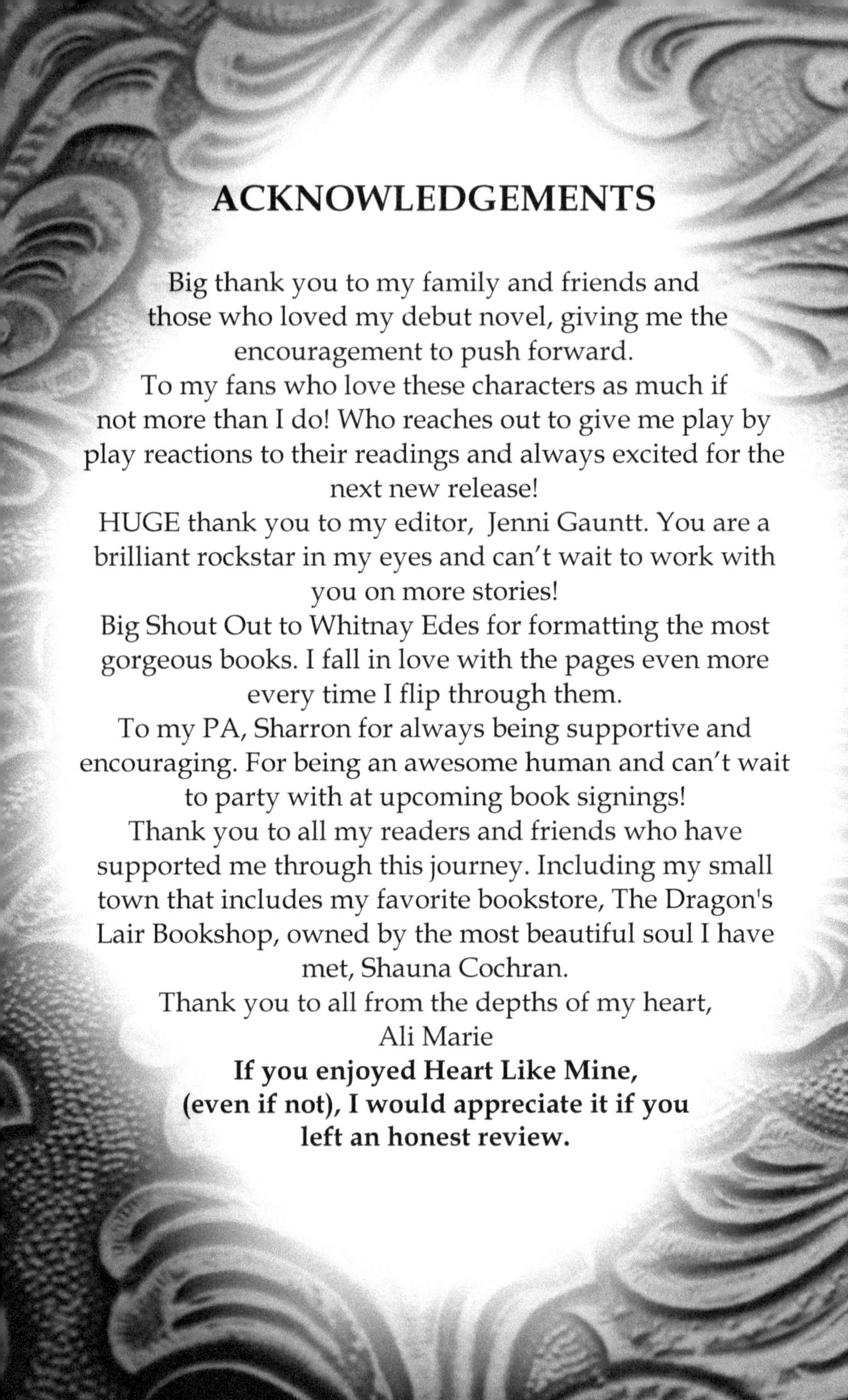

ACKNOWLEDGEMENTS

Big thank you to my family and friends and those who loved my debut novel, giving me the encouragement to push forward.

To my fans who love these characters as much if not more than I do! Who reaches out to give me play by play reactions to their readings and always excited for the next new release!

HUGE thank you to my editor, Jenni Gauntt. You are a brilliant rockstar in my eyes and can't wait to work with you on more stories!

Big Shout Out to Whitnay Edes for formatting the most gorgeous books. I fall in love with the pages even more every time I flip through them.

To my PA, Sharron for always being supportive and encouraging. For being an awesome human and can't wait to party with at upcoming book signings!

Thank you to all my readers and friends who have supported me through this journey. Including my small town that includes my favorite bookstore, The Dragon's Lair Bookshop, owned by the most beautiful soul I have met, Shauna Cochran.

Thank you to all from the depths of my heart,
Ali Marie

**If you enjoyed Heart Like Mine,
(even if not), I would appreciate it if you
left an honest review.**

FOLLOW ME FOR ALL THE FUN AND FOR MORE BOOKS!

https://www.facebook.com/AuthorAliMarie
https://www.instagram.com/alimarie_writelife/
https://www.tiktok.com/@authoralimarie

OTHER BOOKS BY ALI MARIE

Bluebonnet Days

Caught In a Storm - Book 1 of Duet

Heart Novella Series
Heart Like A Truck
Heart Like Mine